# *Introduction*

Fagin, the Artful Dodger, Mr Bumble the beadle and young Oliver Twist himself . . . just four of the unforgettable characters from Charles Dickens' much loved story of the workhouse orphan who dared to say "Please, sir, I want some more."

Generations of children have delighted in the heart-warming adventures of Oliver, who is orphaned as a baby and cruelly brought up in the workhouse. At the age of 9 he runs away to London, where he falls into the hands of the villainous Fagin and his gang.

Terrified by the brutal Sikes, and befriended by Nancy and the roguish Dodger, Oliver seems doomed to a life of crime in the darkest haunts of Victorian London. Yet two strangers come into his life who hold the key to his true identity.

*Oliver Twist* takes the reader back on a historical journey to a London of narrow, bustling lanes, noisy inns and the dark haunts of criminals. By day the streets are full of the well-to-do, street traders, crafty pick pockets and speeding stage coaches. But at night as the ghostly fog creeps up the River Thames, London becomes a place where only scoundrels like Fagin and Sikes venture out.

With his sure touch, master illustrator Eric Kincaid has lovingly recreated Dickens' world – his rich and varied characters and the London they knew.

This edition of Oliver Twist has been carefully abridged to make the text, which was originally written in serial form for a newspaper, the more accessible to young readers.

For young or old, this is a delightful way to enjoy one of Dickens' best-loved tales.

ISBN 0 86112 452 9
This edition © Brimax Books Ltd 1988
All rights reserved
Published by Brimax Books, Newmarket, England
Second printing 1989
Printed in Spain by Graficromo S.A., Cordoba

# OLIVER TWIST

*by*

## CHARLES DICKENS

*Illustrated by* ERIC KINCAID

*Adapted by* PETER OLIVER

BRIMAX BOOKS · NEWMARKET · ENGLAND

## Chapter One

THE strange story of Oliver Twist began a long time ago
in a small town near London. Close to the market square stood
an ugly stone building called the workhouse. It was an unhappy
place where poor people and homeless children were sent to live.
They all laboured from dawn to dusk for just one bowl of soup
each day.

A huge iron gate guarded the entrance and tiny windows
looked down sadly onto the narrow cobbled street below.

A hundred and fifty years ago, in a room behind one of those
windows, a boy was born. It was a bitter winter's night and
outside snow pattered on the window panes. Inside a small fire
burned in the grate and a dim lamp cast shadows across the baby's
face. Two people were talking beside his cot.

'He'll not live. He's too weak,' said Sally, an old nurse at the
workhouse. 'The mother's going fast, too.'

'He won't be the first baby to die in the workhouse,' replied the
surgeon. 'We lost three last week alone.'

But the boy seemed determined to stay alive. He lay gasping

for breath on his mattress and finally let out a loud cry. At that moment a figure stirred beneath a patchwork blanket on a bed in the corner. The pale face of a beautiful girl appeared above the bedclothes. A small gold locket hung at her neck.

'Let me see my child before I die.' It was the boy's mother.

'You must not talk of dying yet,' said the surgeon.

'Lord, bless my heart, no,' cried Sally.

The surgeon took the baby and placed him in the girl's arms. She hugged the child and kissed him warmly on the forehead. Her last wish granted, she looked once more at the baby. Then her head sank back slowly onto the pillow and her eyes closed.

'You were right, Mrs. Thingummy. It's all over,' said the surgeon.

'Ah, poor dear, so it is,' replied Sally, stooping to pick up the boy.

The surgeon told Sally to give the child some soup if it cried. Then he put on his hat and began walking towards the door. Suddenly he stopped, staring curiously at the dead girl.

'She was very good-looking. Where did she come from?' he asked.

Sally shook her head. 'Nobody knows who she is. She was found exhausted on the steps of the workhouse last night. She had walked a long way because her shoes were worn to pieces. But where she came from, or where she was going to, nobody knows.'

The surgeon left and Sally wrapped the boy in a ragged blanket. Nobody looking at him then could have guessed whether he was the son of a nobleman or a beggar. But whichever he was, the baby was now an orphan of the workhouse, to be despised by all and pitied by none.

He cried loudly. If he had known he was an orphan, perhaps he would have cried even louder.

*     *     *     *     *

The news of the birth was given to Mr. Bumble, the beadle. He was the town official responsible for the local poor, or paupers as they were known. A man of little kindness, he wore a high cocked hat and always carried a cane with which to bruise any troublesome children who crossed his path.

Mr. Bumble named the boy Oliver Twist and then took him off to be looked after at the workhouse nursery by Mrs. Mann. She was given seven pence a week to feed and clothe each child. But she did not like to inconvenience the youngsters with too much

food or clothing. The mean and cruel woman would rather take
the money for herself and leave the children to starve.

Yet the heartless Mrs. Mann was no match for Oliver's sturdy
spirit. The boy suffered a loveless childhood but his ninth
birthday found him still alive, though very pale and thin.

Oliver was celebrating his birthday locked in the coal shed
when Mr. Bumble called in to see Mrs. Mann. He was a fat man
and wiped a bead of sweat from his brow after the walk.
'Mrs. Mann,' he said, removing his hat and placing the cane
beside him. 'Oliver Twist is . . .'

Mrs. Mann interrupted him. 'How comes the boy has any name
at all, seeing no one has been able to discover who his father or
mother was?'

'I named him,' said Mr. Bumble proudly. 'I have a system.
I name all our orphans in alphabetical order. The last baby was an
S and I named him Swubble. This was a T and I called him Twist.
The next one that comes will be Unwin and the next Vilkins. I've
got names ready right up to the end of the alphabet.'

Mrs. Mann was very impressed but the beadle went on with his
business. 'Oliver is nine years old today. He's too old to stay here
and must come back to the workhouse to earn his living. So let me
have him at once.'

Oliver was brought in. He was covered in coal dust and held a
little brown cloth cap in his trembling hand. Tears filled his eyes.
Mrs. Mann shook her fist at him. It was the last time her fist
would frighten poor Oliver.

He was taken away from the home where not one kind word or
look had lighted the gloom of his childhood years. Yet he burst
into tears again as the gate closed behind him. The little
companions in misery he was leaving were the only friends he had
ever known. He felt very lonely.

Mr. Bumble, with Oliver hanging onto his gold-laced cuff,
marched back to the workhouse. The Master of the dreadful
place was waiting for him. 'Oliver, you have come here to be
educated and taught a useful trade,' he warned sternly.

'You'll be put to making string from old rope from tomorrow
morning at six o'clock. Now to bed with you.'

Oliver was weak from hunger. But he was sent to his rough,
hard bed without food. He sobbed himself to sleep.

\*       \*       \*       \*       \*

The workhouse was a sad place. The coffin-maker often arrived

to take away children whose hearts had broken with misery. Those who survived childhood did grow up, but they only got hungrier and thinner every day.

The room in which the boys and girls were fed was a large, cold stone hall. A long bare table stood at one end. At the other was a deep copper pot from which the Master, dressed in a white apron, served the gruel. It was watery soup made with a few grains of oatmeal.

The bowls never needed washing up. The children polished them with their spoons until they shone again. Then they sat sucking their fingers, staring hungrily at the copper pot.

Oliver and his companions suffered the tortures of slow starvation for three months. They became desperate with hunger. One of them hinted darkly that he would eat the boy next to him if he didn't have some more food. He had a wild eye and the others believed his threat.

So they decided that someone would have to ask the Master for more to eat. The task fell to Oliver. The next mealtime arrived and the Master served the thin gruel as usual. Then the children whispered among each other and winked at little Oliver.

He rose nervously, his legs shivering in fright. He approached the Master with his bowl and spoon in hand.

'Please, sir, I want some more,' said Oliver.

The Master was a fat, red-faced healthy man, but he turned very pale.

He gazed down in astonishment on the small rebel and clung to the copper pot for support.

'What!' said the Master, in a faint voice.

'Please, sir,' replied Oliver, 'I want some more.'

The Master aimed a blow at Oliver's head with the gruel spoon and shrieked for Mr. Bumble to come.

Mr. Bumble was furious when he heard what had happened. He clipped Oliver sharply around the ankles with his cane. 'Ungracious and ungrateful boy!'

The Master turned to Mr. Bumble and said: 'That boy will be hung one day. I know he will be hung.'

Mr. Bumble would have gladly hung him there and then. Instead he hauled the boy out of the room by his ear and locked him in a windowless room. Oliver was left alone in the dark.

The next day a notice was nailed to the workhouse door. It offered a reward of five pounds to any person who would take Oliver away.

The boy who dared to ask for more food remained a prisoner in

'What!' said the Master, in a faint voice.
'Please, sir,' replied Oliver, 'I want some more.'

his dark cell for a week. He cried bitterly all day. When the long dismal night came on, Oliver spread his hands across his face to shut out the darkness. He crouched in a corner and tried to sleep. But he kept waking with a start and a tremble.

Occasionally Mr. Bumble allowed him to wash under the icy water pump in the yard, warming him up afterwards with strokes of the cane. At night Oliver was flogged again in front of the other children to teach them not to be greedy.

Oliver had yet to learn what kindness meant.

*          *          *          *          *

One morning during Oliver's imprisonment, Mr. Sowerberry, the town coffin-maker, arrived at the workhouse. He met Mr. Bumble at the front gate.

'You'll make your fortune out of the workhouse,' grumbled Mr. Bumble, tapping the man on the shoulder with his cane.

Mr. Sowerberry, a tall, grey man in a threadbare black suit, did not agree. 'The prices you give me for my coffins are very small.'

The Beadle gave a rare smile. 'So are the coffins,' he said.

'There's no denying that,' said Mr. Sowerberry, who seldom smiled. 'Since you feed the children less these days the coffins are somewhat narrower and more shallow than they used to be. But I must have some profit, Mr. Bumble.'

'Indeed, sir,' said Mr. Bumble. 'A fair profit is, of course, allowable. And while I'm on the subject, do you know of anyone who wants a boy? Good terms, I assure you.'

He raised his cane again, pointing at the notice on the door offering Oliver for sale. Mr. Bumble gave three distinct taps on the words FIVE POUNDS.

'Gadso! It was the very thing I wanted to talk to you about,' replied Mr. Sowerberry. 'I need a boy to help me. I'll take him off your hands. Bring him to me tonight.'

That evening Oliver was released from his lonely prison and told he was to become a house lad for the coffin-maker. Mr. Bumble warned him: 'If you complain or ever come back to the workhouse again you will be sent to sea and drowned. Do you hear that, boy!'

Oliver heard the news in silence and went off to pack his worldly possessions. A tiny brown paper parcel held them all. Then, pulling his cap over his eyes and once more attaching himself to Mr. Bumble's cuff, he was led away to a new scene of suffering.

'Oliver!' said Mr. Bumble as they left the workhouse, 'pull that cap off your eyes and hold up your head when you walk.'

Oliver obeyed the order but Mr. Bumble noticed a tear rolling down the boy's cheeks. He stopped and looked fiercely at him. 'Well, of all the most ungrateful boys I have seen . . .'

Oliver protested. 'No, sir,' he said, making sure he clung to the hand which held the cane. 'I will be good, indeed I will, sir. But I am a very little boy and it is so . . . so . . .'

'So . . . what?' inquired Mr. Bumble in amazement.

'So lonely, so very lonely. Everybody hates me. Please, sir, don't be cross with me.'

Mr. Bumble looked at the helpless boy for a moment and cleared his throat. He muttered at Oliver to dry his eyes and be a good boy.

It was dark when they reached the coffin-maker's shop and Mr. Sowerberry and his wife were there to meet them.

'Dear me,' said Mrs. Sowerberry, a penny-pinching woman at the best of times. 'He's very small.' She held a candle closer to get a better view of Oliver.

'There's no denying he's small,' said Mr. Bumble. 'But he'll grow, Mrs. Sowerberry.'

The woman glared at Oliver. 'I dare say he will, but he'll grow on our food and our drink. These boys from the workhouse cost more to keep than they're worth. But my husband thinks he knows best.'

With that, she opened a side door and pushed Oliver down a steep flight of steps into the kitchen. Mrs. Sowerberry followed him down and looked around for some food. The dog had left some of its dinner and that was what Oliver was given. He tore ravenously into the scraps leaving not a morsel.

Mrs. Sowerberry, a short and squeezed-up woman with vixenish eyes, watched in silent horror at Oliver's appetite. Then she picked up a dim and dirty oil lamp and ordered him to follow her. 'Your bed is under the counter in the coffin shop. You don't mind sleeping among the coffins, I suppose?' she said. 'It doesn't matter whether you do or don't. There's nowhere else for you.'

That night Oliver was left alone. The lamp cast frightening shadows. An unfinished coffin stood in the middle of the room and a cold tremble came over him. He expected to see some frightful figure slowly rise out of it and drive him mad with terror.

A row of coffin lids stood against the wall. In the eerie light Oliver thought they were high-shouldered ghosts with hands in their pockets.

He peered at the dark nook beneath the counter where a mattress and a single blanket lay. It looked like a grave. He crept into bed and wished it was his coffin. So alone, Oliver would have been happier lying in a calm and lasting sleep in the churchyard. He could almost imagine the tall grass waving gently above his head and the sound of the old church bell soothing him to sleep.

Oliver shivered and waited for morning to dawn.

## Chapter Two

Oliver was awakened in the morning by a loud kicking at the shop door. 'Open the door, will yer?' cried an angry voice.

'I will directly, sir,' replied Oliver, undoing the door chain and turning the key.

'I suppose you're the new boy, ain't yer?' said the voice through the keyhole.

'Yes, sir,' said Oliver.

'How old are yer?'

'Nearly ten, sir,' replied Oliver.

'Then I'll whop yer when I get in,' said the voice. 'You just see if I don't, work'us brat.'

Oliver drew back the bolts with a trembling hand and opened the door. 'I beg your pardon, sir, did you knock?' he said politely, seeing a boy waiting outside.

'I kicked,' replied the boy.

'Did you want a coffin, sir?' inquired Oliver, innocently.

'You'll want one before long,' said the boy, who looked monstrously fierce. 'You don't know who I am, I suppose, Work'us?'

'No, sir,' said Oliver, realising from the nick-name that the boy knew he had come from the workhouse.

'I'm Mister Noah Claypole and you're my assistant,' said the

boy. 'Now get to work and take down the shutters, yer
idle ruffian!'

With that Noah kicked Oliver and entered the shop with as
much dignity as a boy with a large head, red nose and small
eyes could.

Charlotte, the housekeeper, later gave them breakfast. 'Come
near the fire, Noah,' she said. 'I have saved a nice little bit of
bacon for you. Oliver, your bits are on the bread pan. Take it
away and eat it quickly. Do you hear?'

'D'yer hear, Work'us?' snapped Claypole.

They both looked scornfully at Oliver as he sat shivering in the
coldest corner of the room eating the stale pieces which had been
specially saved for him.

*     *     *     *     *

One day about a month after Oliver had joined the coffin shop,
Mr. Sowerberry was talking to his wife. 'That young Twist, my
dear,' he said. 'A very good looking boy, my dear.'

'He ought to be,' observed Mrs. Sowerberry. 'He eats enough.'

'There's an expression of sadness in his face,' continued
Mr. Sowerberry. 'He would make a delightful mourner to lead
processions at children's funerals. It would have the most
superb effect.'

It was quickly decided that Oliver should be introduced to the
mysteries of the business. Within a few weeks the boy had gained
a great deal of experience.

It was a time when many children were dying from measles and
many were the sad processions which Oliver led, wearing a black
hat with ribbons at the back, which reached down to his knees
and carrying a black stick. The mothers of the town were filled
with admiration for his angelic looks.

But Noah's jealousy was roused at seeing the new boy
promoted to the black stick and hat while he was left in
muffin-cap and leathers. One day at dinner time he was feeling
particularly vicious and took to annoying Oliver.

Noah put his feet on the table cloth and pulled Oliver's hair and
twitched his ears, calling him a sneak. But none of the taunts
made Oliver cry. Noah tried to be nastier still. 'Work'us,' he said,
'how's your mother?'

'She's dead,' replied Oliver. 'Don't you say anything about her
to me!'

'What did she die of, Work'us?' said Noah.

'A broken heart, some of the old nurses told me,' said Oliver. 'I think I know what it must be to die of that.'

'Tol-de-rol, lol-lol, right fol lairy, Work'us,' sneered Noah, spotting a tear roll down Oliver's cheek. 'What's set you snivelling now?'

'Not you!' said Oliver sharply. 'And don't say anything more to me about her; you'd better not.'

'Work'us, don't be impudent,' jeered Noah. 'Your mother was a regular right-down bad'un. It's a great deal better that she died when she did, or else she'd be in prison or hung by now.'

Crimson with fury, Oliver leapt up, overthrew the chair and table and seized Noah by the throat. He shook him with rage until Noah's teeth chattered in his head. Then with one small punch knocked Noah to the ground. Oliver's spirit was roused at last. The cruel insult to his dead mother had set his blood on fire.

Noah screamed for Charlotte. 'Oliver's gone mad! He'll murder me!'

Both Charlotte and Mrs. Sowerberry rushed into the room, one giving Oliver a heavy blow and the other holding him with one hand and scratching his face. The cowardly Noah rose and punched him from behind.

Finally they dragged Oliver, struggling and shouting, into the coal cellar and locked him up.

'Fetch the beadle, Noah,' said Mrs. Sowerberry, 'and tell him to come here immediately.'

Noah ran along the streets at his swiftest pace and found Mr. Bumble at the workhouse. 'Oliver's turned vicious,' said Noah. 'He tried to murder me and then went for Charlotte and Mrs. Sowerberry. Oh what dreadful pain I am in, sir. I am in such agony, please sir.' Noah wasn't even bruised but he wanted as much sympathy as he could get.

Mr. Bumble reached for his cane and hurried off with Noah to the coffin shop. There they found Oliver still kicking from inside the coal cellar.

'Oliver!' said Mr. Bumble.

'Let me out!' replied Oliver.

'Do you know this here voice, Oliver?' threatened the beadle. 'Ain't you afraid of it, ain't you a-trembling as I speak?'

'No, sir,' replied Oliver boldly.

Mr. Bumble staggered and stared in astonishment at the onlookers. Mrs. Sowerberry spoke first. 'Now you know, Mr. Bumble. He must be mad. No boy in his right senses would speak to a beadle like that.'

'It's not madness, ma'am,' exclaimed Mr. Bumble. 'It's meat! You've overfed him. If you had kept him on gruel, ma'am, this would never have happened.'

'Dear me!' exclaimed the woman, who had in truth only fed Oliver on the dirty odds and ends which nobody else would eat. 'This comes of being too generous.'

At that moment Mr. Sowerberry returned. As soon as he heard the news, he unlocked the cellar door and dragged his rebellious boy out by the collar.

Oliver's clothes had been torn in the beating he had received, his face was bruised and scratched and his hair was scattered over his forehead. 'Now, you are a nice young fellow, ain't you,' said Mr. Sowerberry, giving the boy a shake and a box on the ear.

'He called my mother names,' said Oliver, scowling boldly at Noah.

'Well, and what if he did, you little ungrateful wretch,' said Mrs. Sowerberry. 'She deserved what he said, and worse.'

'It's a lie,' said Oliver furiously.

The remark earned him another beating, this time from Mr. Sowerberry.

It wasn't the last. Mr. Bumble's cane did its worst before Oliver was finally sent to bed.

It was not until he was left alone in the silence and stillness of the gloomy coffin shop that Oliver gave way to his feelings. He had listened to everyone's taunts with a look of contempt and suffered the cane without a cry. But now, where no one could see him, Oliver fell on his knees and wept.

For a long time he remained motionless. The candle was burning low when he rose to his feet. He looked cautiously around him, listened intently and then quietly opened the door and looked out into the night. It was cold and dark outside. He shut the door again and, in the dying light of the candle, he put the few clothes he owned into a handkerchief and waited for morning.

When the first rays of light struggled through the shutters, Oliver rose and again unbarred the door. In an instant he was in the street. He looked to the right and then to the left, uncertain in which direction to fly. He decided to take the route up the hill where he'd seen the wagons go. Soon he found a footpath across some fields. He recognised it as the way Mr. Bumble had taken him back to the workhouse from the nursery.

At the nursery he stopped and looked over the wall into the garden. It was still very early but already a child was weeding the

beds. It was Dick, the little boy who had been beaten, starved and shut up with Oliver many a time.

'Dick!' cried Oliver, as the boy ran to the wall and thrust his thin arm forward to greet him. 'Is anyone else about?'

'Nobody but me,' said Dick.

'You mustn't say you saw me,' said Oliver. 'I am running away. They beat and ill-used me, Dick. I am going to seek my fortune some long way off. I don't know where.'

'It's good to see you, Oliver,' said Dick. 'But don't stop. You must hurry.'

The boy climbed up the low wall and flung his arms around Oliver. 'Goodbye, Oliver. And God bless you.'

'I shall see you again, Dick,' said Oliver. 'I know I shall. And when I do you will be well and happy.'

It was a sad farewell and one that Oliver never forgot.

## Chapter Three

OLIVER was nearly five miles away from the town by eight o'clock. He had run and hidden behind hedges all the way, frightened he might be chased and overtaken. Then he sat down by a milestone and began to think for the first time about where he might go and try to live.

The stone told him it was seventy miles to London. 'London, that great place,' he thought. 'Not even Mr. Bumble could find me there!'

He set off again, counting his possessions. All he had was a crust of bread, a rough shirt and two pairs of darned socks. In his pocket was a penny, a gift from Mr. Sowerberry after performing well at a recent funeral.

Oliver walked twenty miles that day, eating just the crust of dry bread and begging some water at cottages on the road. When night came, he crept under a haystack to sleep. He felt frightened at first as the wind moaned over the empty fields. He was very cold and hungry and felt more alone than ever before. But he was very tired from his walk and soon fell asleep.

The next morning a stagecoach came up and Oliver begged the passengers sitting on top of it for a lift. But they took little notice of him and the coach rattled away in a cloud of dust. Oliver might well have died that day but for the kindness of a roadmender who gave him some bread and cheese and an old lady who took pity on him.

And so Oliver continued on to London. Early on the seventh day after running away he limped into the little town of Barnet, a few miles from the city. Oliver, with bleeding feet, sat down on a cold doorstep to rest. He had been crouching there for some time watching the passing coaches when he saw a boy looking at him from the other side of the road.

'Hello, my covey, what's the trouble?' the boy said, getting up to walk across to Oliver.

The boy, about the same age as Oliver, was one of the oddest looking Oliver had ever seen. He was short, snub-nosed, sharp-eyed and had the air and manners of a grown-up man. He wore a man's coat which reached nearly to his heels. The cuffs were turned up to let his arms out of his sleeves. He was altogether as roystering and swaggering a young gentleman as ever stood four feet six high.

'What's the trouble, my friend?' he repeated.

'I am very tired and hungry,' replied Oliver. 'I have walked a long way.'

'Going to London?' said the strange boy.

'Yes,' said Oliver.

'I suppose you want somewhere to sleep tonight?'

Oliver agreed again. 'I have not slept under a roof since I left the country.'

'Don't you worry yourself,' said the boy. 'I've got to be in London tonight and I know a respectable gentleman who lives there, wot'll give us lodging for nothing.'

The unexpected offer of shelter was too tempting to be resisted. 'That would be kind,' said Oliver.

'Then I'm your man,' said the boy, before revealing his identity. 'Jack Dawkins the name, or to my more intimate friends, the Artful Dodger.'

As Oliver's new friend strangely objected to their entering London before nightfall, it was nearly eleven o'clock before they reached the city. The Dodger hurried through the streets with

Oliver close at his heels.

They reached a place called Saffron Hill. Oliver had never seen a dirtier or more wretched place. The street was very narrow and muddy. The air was full of bad smells and children running around and screaming even at that time of night. Drunken men and women staggered around in the filth.

Oliver was just considering whether he shouldn't have run away after all when they reached the bottom of the hill. The Dodger pushed open the door of a house and pulled him into a passage.

'Who's there?' cried a voice.

'Plummy and slam,' replied Dodger.

Oliver didn't understand but took the words to be some password or signal. A feeble candle gleamed from the end of the dark passage and a man's face appeared out of the shadow.

'Is Fagin upstairs?' asked the Dodger.

'Yes, he's sorting out the handkerchiefs,' said a voice. The candle and the face disappeared.

The Dodger grasped Oliver's hand and led him up a set of broken stairs and into a room. The walls and ceiling were perfectly black with age and dirt. A candle, stuck in a beer bottle, glimmered on a table. Seated around it were four or five boys, none older than Oliver, smoking long clay pipes and drinking beer with the air of middle-aged men.

By a crackling fire, a very old and shrivelled man was cooking some sausages in a frying pan. His villainous and ugly face was partly hidden by a beard of matted red hair. Dressed in a greasy flannel gown, he was dividing his attention between the sausages and a great number of silk handkerchiefs drying on a clothes-horse.

'This is my friend Oliver Twist,' said Dodger. 'I met him on the road.'

The old man grinned nastily and made a low bow to Oliver. The other boys gathered round and shook his hand.

'We are very glad to see you, Oliver . . . very glad, my dear,' said the man. 'My name is Mr. Fagin. Now, Dodger, take off the sausages and draw up a chair for Oliver.'

Fagin saw Oliver staring at the handkerchiefs. 'There are a good many of 'em, ain't there?' he said. 'We've just got 'em out ready to wash; that's all Oliver, that's all. Ha! Ha! Ha!'

The other boys joined in the boisterous laughter and then began their supper. Oliver ate his share ravenously. Fagin mixed him a glass of gin and water and told him to drink it in one go.

*'This is my friend Oliver Twist,'*
*said Dodger. 'I met him on the road.'*

Oliver did as he was told and immediately afterwards felt very drowsy. He dimly remembered being lifted onto a comfortably stuffed sack, where he sank into a deep sleep.

\*        \*        \*        \*        \*

Oliver awoke late the next morning. Between his half-closed eyes he saw that Fagin was the only person in the room. The old man was crouched over several boxes. Oliver watched him shrugging his shoulders in delight. His face was distorted with a hideous grin. The boxes were overflowing with gold watches, rings, brooches, bracelets, and other jewellery.

Fagin was muttering to himself when he saw Oliver's eyes on him. He slammed the boxes shut and reached for a bread knife on the table. Oliver saw the knife quiver in the air.

'What do you watch me for, boy?' said Fagin furiously. 'Why are you awake? What have you seen? Speak out, boy! Quick, quick, for your life, boy.'

Oliver replied meekly: 'I wasn't able to sleep any longer, sir. I am very sorry if I disturbed you, sir.'

Fagin laid his hand on one of the boxes. 'Did you see any of these pretty things?' he asked.

'Yes, sir,' replied Oliver.

'Ah,' said Fagin, turning rather pale. 'They . . . they're mine, Oliver. My little property . . . all I have to live on in my old age. The folks call me a miser, my dear – only a miser; that's all.'

Oliver thought the old gentleman must be a miser to live in such a dirty place with so many watches and pieces of jewellery. But he took little notice of what he'd seen and got up to wash. By the time he had finished, Dodger and another of the boys had returned. The four sat down to a breakfast of coffee and some hot rolls and ham. Dodger had brought back the food hidden in the crown of his hat.

'Well,' said Fagin, glancing slyly at Oliver, but talking to Dodger, 'I hope you've been hard at work this morning. What have you got, my dears?'

Dodger answered first. 'A couple of wallets,' he said, handing them over to Fagin.

'Not so heavy as they might be,' said Fagin, after looking at the insides very carefully, 'but very neat and nicely made. Clever workman, Dodger, ain't he, Oliver?'

'Very good workman, indeed,' said the innocent Oliver. The second boy, Charley Bates, laughed at Oliver's answer.

'And what have you got, my dear?' Fagin asked Charley.
'Handkerchiefs,' he replied.

'Well,' smiled Fagin, examining them closely. 'They're very
good ones.' He turned to Oliver and said: 'You'd like to be able
to make handkerchiefs as easily as Charley, wouldn't you,
my dear?'

'Very much, sir, if you would teach me,' said Oliver.

Charley burst into laughter again. He nearly choked on
his coffee.

After breakfast Fagin and the boys played a very curious game.
The old man placed a snuff box in one trouser pocket, a wallet in
the other, a watch in his waistcoat, a diamond pin in his shirt and
a handkerchief in a back pocket. Then he trotted up and down the
room with a stick, imitating the way old gentlemen walk about
the streets.

Sometimes he stopped at the fireplace and sometimes at the
door, making believe that he was staring at a shop window. He
constantly looked around him, imagining thieves. All the while
the two boys followed him around. At last Dodger trod on his
toes and Charley stumbled against him. In one instant they
snatched with extraordinary speed all the items that he had
hidden on himself. The game was repeated time and time again.
If Fagin ever felt a hand in any of his pockets, he would cry out
and the game would begin once again.

Oliver was very puzzled, even more so when Charley said it was
time to pad the hoof. Oliver thought it must be French for going
out because Dodger and Charley left soon after.

Fagin then asked Oliver whether his handkerchief was hanging
out of his pocket. 'Yes, sir,' said Oliver.

'See if you can take it out without my feeling it,' said Fagin.

Oliver copied what he had seen Dodger do and held the
handkerchief with one hand and drew it out gently with the other.

'Is it gone?' cried the old man.

'Here it is, sir,' said Oliver proudly.

'You're a clever boy, my dear,' said the playful old gentleman.
'I never saw a sharper lad. Here's a shilling for you. If you go on
this way you'll be the greatest man of our time.'

Oliver wondered what picking Fagin's pocket had to do with his
chances of being a great man.

*     *     *     *     *

For many days Oliver stayed in Fagin's house, playing the strange game every morning. Then one day Oliver was told to go out with Dodger and Charley.

The three boys sallied out. The Dodger had his coat sleeves tucked up and his hat cocked as usual. Charley walked with his hands in his pockets. As they emerged from a narrow court Dodger made a sudden stop.

'What's the matter?' asked Oliver.

'Hush!' said Dodger. 'Do you see that old gent at the bookstall?'

'Yes, I see him.'

'He'll do,' said Dodger to Charley.

The two boys walked stealthily across the road and slunk up behind the old man. Oliver looked on in silent amazement.

The man was a very respectable person with gold spectacles. He was dressed in a bottle green coat with a black velvet collar and wore white trousers. He carried a smart bamboo cane under his arm and was reading something at the bookstall.

Oliver's eyes opened wide as he saw the Dodger plunge his hand into the man's pocket and draw out a handkerchief. He handed it to Charley and then they both ran off around the corner at top speed.

In an instant the whole mystery of the handkerchiefs, the watches, the jewels and Fagin himself became clear to Oliver. He stood for a moment with the blood tingling through his veins in terror. Confused and frightened he took to his heels and made off as fast as he could.

In the very instant Oliver set off, the old gentleman put his hand in his pocket and discovered his handkerchief was missing. He turned sharply around. Seeing Oliver scudding away at such a rapid pace, the man automatically assumed he was the villain. 'Stop thief!' he cried, giving chase.

Dodger and Charley heard the shout and returned to the scene. Like good citizens they cried 'stop thief' too and joined the chase after Oliver.

Down the street they all ran, pell-mell, helter-skelter, slap-dash, tearing, yelling and screaming 'Stop thief! Stop thief!'

Oliver didn't get far. He was tackled and brought down on the pavement. The crowd eagerly gathered around him. 'Stand aside' . . . 'Give him a little air!' . . . 'Nonsense, he don't deserve it!' Everyone had something to say.

Oliver lay covered with mud and dust and was bleeding from his mouth. The old gentleman reached the scene. 'Poor young

*Oliver's eyes opened wide as he saw
Dodger plunge his hand into the man's pocket.*

fellow,' he said with a kind face. 'He's hurt himself.'

At that moment a police officer arrived and seized Oliver by his collar.

'It wasn't me sir, it was two other boys,' said Oliver. 'They are here somewhere.'

'Oh no they ain't,' said the officer. 'Come along, get up.'

The old gentleman interrupted. 'Don't hurt him,' he said with sympathy.

'Oh, I won't hurt him,' replied the officer, tearing Oliver's jacket half off his back. 'Stand up, you young devil!'

Oliver finally got to his feet and was dragged down the street by his jacket collar. The old gentleman followed the unhappy boy all the way to the local police courthouse.

Behind them skulked a mysterious man, almost hidden in a huge black cloak. His eyes stared at Oliver in disbelief. 'I've found him!' he muttered in a horrible whisper.

Oliver didn't see the man then and it would be several months before he did.

## Chapter Four

OLIVER was led into a cold stone police cell. The old gentleman looked on thoughtfully as the key turned in the lock.

'There is something in that boy's face,' he said to himself, walking towards the court room, 'something that touches me. Where have I seen something like that face before?'

He thought of all the people he had ever known. But he could not recall any face which reminded him of Oliver, and soon he was ushered into the presence of the magistrate, the renowned Mr. Fang.

Mr. Fang was a lean, long-backed, stiff-necked man with just a little hair growing at the back and sides of his head. His face was stern and flushed from drinking too much gin.

'Who are you?' said Mr. Fang, scowling angrily.

'My name, sir, is Brownlow,' replied the gentleman.

'What is he charged with?' said Mr. Fang, turning to the court officer.

'He's not charged with anything,' said the officer. 'It's the boy. Pick-pocketing.'

Mr. Fang knew all too well but he felt like annoying the kindly old man.

Oliver was brought in and placed in a wooden pen. Mr. Brownlow looked at him and then spoke to Mr. Fang. 'I am not sure this boy actually took my handkerchief. I would rather not press the case against him.'

'Hold your tongue!' snapped Mr. Fang.

'I will not, sir,' said Mr. Brownlow indignantly.

'Hold your tongue this instant, or I'll have you removed from the court,' said Mr. Fang. 'How dare you bully a magistrate!'

Just then Oliver, trembling and looking very pale, asked for a drink of water. 'Stuff and nonsense,' said Mr. Fang. 'You don't need water!'

'I think he really is ill,' said the court officer.

'I know better,' said Mr. Fang. 'He's a hardened scoundrel, a young vagabond.'

Mr. Brownlow interrupted. 'Take care of the boy. He'll fall.'

'Let him fall, if he likes,' said Mr. Fang.

Oliver collapsed onto the floor in a fainting fit but still Mr. Fang felt no sympathy. 'Let him lie there, he'll soon be tired of that.'

Mr. Fang wasted no more time. 'The boy is guilty and I sentence him to three months hard labour. Now clear the court.'

At that moment an elderly man rushed into the court. Mr. Fang was furious. 'What's this?' he cried. 'Turn the man out. Clear the office!'

'I will not be turned out,' said the man. 'I will speak. I saw everything that happened. The robbery was committed by another boy.'

Mr. Fang paused and listened to the man telling how he had seen Dodger and Charley take the handkerchief and run off. Then he announced to the court: 'The wretched boy appears to be innocent. Let him go.'

Oliver was carried out of the court and laid on the pavement.

'Poor boy,' said Mr. Brownlow, bending over him. 'Call a coach, someone. I must take him home.'

*     *     *     *     *

Oliver was taken by coach to Mr. Brownlow's home in Pentonville, a well-to-do area of London. He was put to bed immediately and the doctor called. For many days the boy remained in a fever, unaware of the kindness and love which he was receiving.

Weak and thin, Oliver at last awoke from what seemed to have been a long and troubled dream. 'What room is this? Where am I?' he said, feebly raising himself up.

Mr. Brownlow's kindly housekeeper, Mrs. Bedwin, was by his bedside. 'Hush, my dear. You must be very quiet or you will be ill again. You have been very sick.'

With those words the lady very gently placed Oliver's head back on the pillow. She looked so kindly and lovingly in his face, that Oliver could not help placing a little withered hand on hers.

'What a grateful little dear he is,' said Mrs. Bedwin. 'What would his mother feel if she could see him now?'

Oliver spoke again. 'Perhaps she does see me,' he whispered. 'Perhaps she has sat with me. I almost feel as if she had.'

'That was the fever,' said Mrs. Bedwin.

'I suppose it was,' said Oliver. 'Heaven is a long way away and they are too happy there to come down to the bedside of a poor boy. If she had seen me hurt it would have made her sorrowful, and her face has always looked sweet and happy when I have dreamed of her.'

*       *       *       *       *

Within a few days Oliver had recovered from the fever and Mrs. Bedwin had him carried downstairs to sit in her room. She gave him some soup, strong enough to feed three hundred and fifty boys in the workhouse. As Oliver ate, his eyes fell on a portrait of a lady hanging on the wall.

'What a beautiful face that lady has,' said Oliver. 'Who is she?'

'Why, really, my dear, I don't know,' said Mrs. Bedwin. 'I don't expect it's anyone you or I know. It seems to strike your fancy.'

'It makes my heart beat quickly,' said Oliver. 'The eyes look so sorrowful and they seem fixed on me. It's as if the portrait was alive and wanted to speak to me but couldn't.'

Their conversation was interrupted by the arrival of Mr. Brownlow. 'How do you feel, young man?' he asked.

'Very happy, sir,' replied Oliver. 'And very grateful for your kindness to me.'

Mr. Brownlow was asking whether Oliver had been fed when he suddenly stopped and stared at the hanging portrait. 'Why! What's this? Bedwin, look here.'

Mr Brownlow pointed to the picture and then to the boy's face. It was a living copy. The eyes, the head, the mouth were precisely alike. Every feature was the same.

## Chapter Five

'**W**HERE'S Oliver?' said Fagin, glaring menacingly at Dodger and Charley.

The young thieves had returned to Fagin's dark lair and were now looking uneasily at each other.

'What's become of the boy?' said Fagin, seizing the Dodger tightly by the coat collar. 'Speak up or I'll throttle you!'

'The police got him and that's all I know,' said Dodger. 'Come on, let me go!'

'What!' thundered Fagin. 'He'll tell the police everything and we'll all be done for.'

Dodger was so scared, he swung around. In one jerk he was clean out of his coat, which was left swinging in Fagin's hands. Fagin dropped the garment and picked up a pot and threw it at Dodger. He ducked as it flew towards his head.

At that moment the door opened and the pot crashed into the wall, narrowly missing a man coming into the room. It was Bill Sikes, Fagin's partner in crime.

'What the blazes is going on?' stormed Sikes, a stoutly built man of thirty-five years. He was wearing a black coat, dirty breeches and lace-up knee-length boots. A brown hat shaded his cruel face and a filthy handkerchief was tied around his neck. He had a black eye from a recent fight. 'Ill-treating the boys again . . . I wonder they don't murder you.'

Behind him skulked a white dog with blood red eyes. Its face

was scratched and torn. 'Come on, Fagin. What's going on?' he repeated, kicking the dog into the corner of the room. The animal was clearly used to such treatment and coiled himself up in a corner without uttering a sound.

'I'm afraid,' said Fagin, 'that Dodger and Charley have brought news which might get us all into trouble and if the game's up, you'll come off worse than me.'

'You snivelling, white-livered, old thief,' said Sikes fiercely. 'If you was a dog I'd kill you now! What's up?'

Fagin told Sikes the story of what had happened. 'Oliver must be found and brought back,' said Sikes. 'Or else we'll all be hung. My Nancy will be here soon. She'll help.'

\*       \*       \*       \*       \*

A plan was arranged. Sikes' girl Nancy was to go to the courthouse and find out what happened to Oliver. She was to pretend that Oliver was her brother who had run away from home.

Nancy was scared but she finally agreed to the scheme after being threatened by both Sikes and Fagin. She returned later that day with the news that Oliver had been released by the court and was taken away in a coach by a Mr. Brownlow. She had spoken to a man who had overheard the coach driver being given instructions to drive to Pentonville.

Fagin knew what had to be done. 'He must be kidnapped. But first he must be found,' said Fagin. 'Dodger, Charley. You must do nothing but skulk about the streets until you find some news of him. Nancy, you must help. Oliver must be found.'

\*       \*       \*       \*       \*

The days that followed were happy days for Oliver. Everybody was so kind and gentle. After all the sadness and cruelty which had followed him, his life at Mr. Brownlow's house was like Heaven itself. The old man's heart was big enough for six people.

One evening he asked Oliver to do him a favour. He wanted some books returned to a bookshop and some money taken to pay a bill.

Oliver was delighted to be able to return some of Mr. Brownlow's kindness. 'I won't be ten minutes,' said Oliver hurrying out of the house with the books under his arms and a five pound note in his pocket.

Mrs. Bedwin anxiously watched him go. 'I can't bear to let him out of my sight,' she said.

Oliver did not know the streets of London very well and took a wrong turning on his way to the bookshop. He did not discover his mistake until he was half way down, but knowing that it must lead in the right direction, he didn't think it was worthwhile turning back.

He walked along thinking how content and happy he was. Suddenly he was startled by a young woman screaming out very loud: 'Oh, my dear brother!' Oliver hardly had time to look up before a pair of arms were thrown tightly round his neck.

'Don't,' cried Oliver, struggling. 'Let me go.'

But the woman continued to cry out. 'Oh, my gracious! I've found my brother. Oh, you naughty boy! How you made me suffer. Come home now.'

'What's the matter?' asked a passer-by, seeing Oliver struggle.

'He ran away from his parents a month ago,' said the woman holding Oliver. 'He joined a set of thieves and almost broke his mother's heart.'

'The young wretch,' the man replied, turning to Oliver. 'Go home, you brute.'

Oliver became alarmed. 'I don't know her,' he cried. 'I haven't any sister, father or mother. I'm an orphan and live at Pentonville.'

But it was hopeless. The next moment a man burst out of a nearby beerhouse with a white dog at his heels. 'Young Oliver,' he said. 'Come home to your poor mother, you young dog.'

Oliver kept struggling. 'I don't belong to them,' he shouted. 'Help! Help!'

'Come on, you young villain,' threatened the man, seizing Oliver by the collar and calling his dog. 'Here Bull's-eye! Mind the boy!'

Weak from his recent illness and stunned by the sudden attack, Oliver was terrified by the fierce growling of the dog and the brutality of the man. What could one poor child do? Darkness had set in and it was an area full of criminals. There was no help to be had. Resistance was useless.

Soon he was being dragged forcibly along a maze of dark narrow streets. His cries went unheard.

\*　　　\*　　　\*　　　\*　　　\*

Outside Mr. Brownlow's house the gas lights were lit. Mrs. Bedwin waited anxiously at the open door. Where was Oliver?

\*       \*       \*       \*       \*

Sikes, Nancy, the dog Bull's-eye and their prisoner, Oliver, finally stopped for breath near London's Smithfield Market. Nancy was unable to keep up the fierce pace they had walked since leaving the scene of the kidnap.

'Take hold of Nancy's hand, Oliver, do you hear,' growled Sikes, 'and give me the other.'

Sikes called Bull's-eye over and put his hand to Oliver's throat. 'If you speak even a word, that's where the dog will put his teeth,' he warned.

They walked on through the dark and foggy night. The streets and houses were shrouded in gloom. They had gone on a few paces when the church bell struck eight o'clock. It was the hour that condemned criminals in Newgate Gaol were taken from their cells to be hanged.

Oliver felt Nancy's hand tremble. He looked up into her face and saw that it had turned deadly white. She feared it was the hour that Sikes would one day end his life.

They reached Fagin's den and Dodger opened the door. 'Toll-de-loll, gammon and spinnage!' he laughed. 'It's Oliver come back.' He led the way upstairs with the help of a gleaming candle stuck in the end of a split stick.

Charley Bates greeted them at the top with a shout of laughter. 'Look at his togs,' he roared, pointing out the new suit that Mr. Brownlow had bought him. 'Nothing but a real gentleman.'

Fagin appeared out of a dark corner. 'Delighted to see you looking so well, Oliver, my dear,' he said, bowing with mock humility. 'The Dodger will give you another suit for fear that you spoil that Sunday best one you're wearing. Why didn't you write and say you were coming? We'd have got something warm for supper.'

Charley laughed again and even the Dodger smiled. His clever fingers had already found the five pound note that Mr. Brownlow had intended for the bookseller.

Oliver looked at his tormentors. 'Please. The money belongs to the old gentleman,' he pleaded. 'Please send the money back. Keep me here all my life but send the money back. He'll think I stole it.'

*They walked on through the dark and foggy
night. The streets and houses were shrouded in gloom.*

Oliver fell at Fagin's feet. But the evil man was thinking. He knitted his shaggy red eyebrows into a hard knot and announced: 'You're right, Oliver. You're right! They will think you have stolen it. Ha! Ha!'

Fagin chuckled and rubbed his hands in glee. 'It couldn't have happened better. He will think you're a thief!'

Oliver jumped to his feet and tore wildly out of the room, shrieking for help. His cries echoed to the leaking roof. Sikes called to Bull's-eye.

'Keep back the dog, Bill,' screamed Nancy, closing the door as Fagin and his two pupils darted out in pursuit. 'Keep back the dog. He'll tear the boy to pieces.'

'Serve him right,' snarled Sikes, struggling to get out of the girl's grasp. 'Stand away from me or I'll split your head against the wall.'

'I don't care,' she answered. 'The child won't be torn down by the dog unless you kill me first.'

'I'll soon do that if you don't keep away,' said Sikes, his teeth set fiercely. With that he flung the girl to the floor. But just then Fagin and the boys returned with Oliver.

'What's the matter here?' said Fagin.

'The girl's gone mad,' replied Sikes.

'No I haven't,' said Nancy. 'Don't you think it.'

Fagin turned his attention to Oliver. 'So you wanted to get away, did you, my dear,' he sneered, picking up a heavy and knotted log lying by the fireplace. 'Wanted to call the police, did you? We'll soon cure you of that, young master.'

Fagin hit Oliver sharply over the shoulder and was raising the club for a second blow when Nancy rushed forward and grabbed it.

She threw it into the fire. 'I won't stand by and see it done, Fagin. You've got the boy and what more would you have? Let Oliver be. From tonight you'll make him a liar and a thief. Isn't that enough?'

Nancy stamped her foot violently on the floor as her anger exploded. 'You made me a thief when I was half Oliver's age and I've been in the same business for you ever since. It's my living now, just as the cold, wet and dirty streets are my home. And you're the evil man who brought me here.'

Fagin refused to take any more from Nancy. 'I shall do you a mischief if you don't stop.'

The girl said nothing but made a frenzied rush at Fagin. Sikes caught her just in time to save the old man. She struggled

a moment and then fainted. 'She'll be all right now,' said Sikes.

'Charley,' called Fagin. 'Put Oliver to bed.'

'I suppose he'd better not wear his best clothes tomorrow, had he?' asked Charley.

'Certainly not,' replied Fagin, a horrible grin crossing his face.

Oliver was locked up for the night and, sick and weary, soon fell asleep. He dreamed of little Dick in the nursery.

## Chapter Six

A few days later, close to where Oliver was imprisoned, a fat beadle tucked into a meal of steak, oyster sauce and wine. Mr. Bumble had arrived in London on business the day before. His stomach was full, he drew his chair to the fire and began reading the newspaper. His eye was quickly drawn to an advertisement:

*Five Guineas Reward*
*The above reward will be paid to any person who can give any information about a boy called Oliver Twist who ran away, or was kidnapped, on Thursday evening last from his house at Pentonville.*

Beneath it was the name and address of Mr. Brownlow. Mr. Bumble was astounded and within five minutes was on his way. At Mr. Brownlow's house he knocked on the door.

Mrs. Bedwin answered the door. 'Is Mr. Brownlow at home?' said the beadle. 'I have some information about Oliver Twist.'

'Come in, come in,' said Mrs. Bedwin. 'I knew we should hear news of him, the poor dear.'

Soon he was sitting with Mr. Brownlow. 'Do you know where the boy is now?' asked the kindly old gentleman.

'No more than nobody,' said Mr. Bumble.

Mr. Brownlow was anxious. 'Well, what do you know of him?

Speak out if you have anything to say.'

Mr. Bumble put down his hat, unbuttoned his coat and began the story that he liked best. Oliver had been born of vicious parents and since his birth had shown nothing but treachery, ingratitude and malice. Indeed, he had made a cowardly attack on an innocent poor boy and run away from his master's house.

'I fear it is all true,' said Mr. Brownlow sadly. 'I would have gladly given you three times the reward if you had brought me good news about the boy.'

Mr. Bumble would have told a different story if he'd known that. But now it was too late. Mr. Brownlow gave the beadle his five guineas and rang the bell for Mrs. Bedwin to come.

'Mrs. Bedwin, Oliver is an imposter,' he said sternly.

'He can't be, sir,' pleaded the housekeeper. 'I will never believe it. He was a dear child and I know what children are and I have done for forty years.'

'Silence, Mrs. Bedwin,' said the old man. 'Never let me hear the boy's name again.'

There were sad hearts at the Brownlow's house that night.

*     *     *     *     *

When Oliver awoke the next morning Fagin was ready to give the boy a stern lecture about his future. 'You don't want to hang, do you?' said Fagin, putting a hand to his throat and dropping his shoulders in imitation of the rope doing its work.

Little Oliver's blood ran cold. Fagin smiled hideously and patted Oliver on the head. 'If you are a good boy and work for me, you won't,' he continued. 'If you keep your mouth shut and obey me we can still be good friends. Do you understand?'

Fagin left the room and locked the door behind him. Oliver was left in the room for several days eating and sleeping alone, but after a week the door was unlocked. Oliver was free to wander about the house. He was too terrified to think of escaping. When Fagin and the boys were out he would sit in a room high up in the house, gazing out of a barred window. Huge spiders' webs hung from the glass and mice scurried about the room.

For hours he would sadly stare out at the crowded mass of roof tops and blackened chimneys.

One evening when the boys had returned, Dodger asked Oliver to clean his boots. Oliver was only too happy to be of some use.

'Why don't you work for Fagin?' asked Dodger, watching Oliver kneeling at his feet, polishing his boots. 'You could make a fortune. It's a jolly life.'

'I don't like to steal,' replied Oliver timidly. 'I wish he would let me go.'

'Fagin won't do that,' said Dodger. 'But he'll make something of you, or you'll be the first boy he ever failed with. So you might as well join our gang.'

From that day Oliver was seldom left alone. Dodger and Charley spent most days with him and at night Fagin would tell stories of robberies he had done in his earlier years.

It was all a plan. Fagin was determined to poison Oliver's mind and blacken his character for ever.

\* \* \* \* \*

Fagin began Oliver's education into the ways of crime. Sikes was to complete it. He was planning a robbery at a big house in the country. But he needed a small boy to help. Fagin suggested Oliver. 'It's time he began to work for his bread,' Fagin told Sikes. 'And besides, once he's done a job with you he'll know he's a thief. And then he's ours. Ours for life!'

The old man crossed his arms over his chest and, drawing his head and shoulders into a heap, hugged himself for joy. Oliver was almost in his power.

When Fagin got home that night he went to Oliver's bedroom and told him that Nancy would arrive later to take him to Sikes.

'Why am I going?' asked Oliver anxiously.

'You don't know?' asked Fagin.

Oliver shook his head. 'Bah!' said Fagin, disappointed at the boy's innocence. 'Wait till Mr. Sikes tells you.'

The old man walked to the door and then stopped. 'Take heed, Oliver,' he said, shaking his bony finger at the boy. 'Take heed. Mr. Sikes is a rough man and thinks nothing of killing little boys. Whatever happens, say nothing, and do whatever he asks.'

Fagin left and Oliver opened a book which the old thief had asked him to read. It was a history of the lives of famous criminals.

Oliver read of dreadful crimes, of secret murders on lonely lanes and bodies hidden in deep wells. The terrible descriptions were so real and vivid that the pages of the book seemed to run red with blood. In a fit of fear Oliver shut the book and threw it aside. He got out of bed and fell on his knees, praying to Heaven to spare him from such horrible deeds.

He had finished his prayers when a figure appeared at the door.

'Who's that?' he cried with a start.

'Only me.' It was Nancy. 'Are you ready?'

'Why am I going to Mr. Sikes?' asked the boy.

'You won't be harmed,' said Nancy.

'I don't believe it,' said Oliver.

'Hush!' replied Nancy. 'You can't help yourself. I've tried hard for you. I've saved you from being beaten once and I will again. But I've promised that you'll be good. If you're not, you'll only harm yourself and me too. You might be my death.'

Oliver looked at Nancy's face and could see that she spoke the truth. He didn't want her harmed. 'If I could help you, I would, but I can't at the moment,' said Nancy. 'They don't mean to harm you and remember that whatever they make you do, its not your fault. Now give me your hand. We must go.'

Outside there was a horse-drawn cab waiting. Nancy pulled Oliver into it and drew the curtains across the windows. Instantly the driver lashed his horse into full speed. Soon they were at Sikes' house and climbed out of the cab.

For one brief moment Oliver glanced along the empty street. A cry for help hung on his lips. But he remembered Nancy's words and lost the heart to shout out.

While he hesitated, his chance of escape was lost. Oliver was taken into the house and the door shut behind him.

'Did he come quiet?' inquired Sikes.

'Like a lamb,' said Nancy.

'I'm glad to hear it,' said Sikes, looking grimly at Oliver. 'Now come here, young 'un. I want to give you a lecture.'

Sikes sat down at a table and stood the boy in front of him. 'Now, do you know what this is?' he asked, pulling a pistol from his pocket.

'Yes,' said Oliver, trembling.

Sikes grasped Oliver's wrists tightly and put the barrel against his temple. 'When we leave here you mustn't say a word unless I speak to you. If you do I'll blow your head off. Understand?'

Oliver understood only too well.

*     *     *     *     *

Oliver slept little that night. When he woke up it was almost dawn and Sikes was dressed and ready to go.

'Now then,' he growled. 'Half past five! Look sharp. We've got a long way to go.'

Oliver dressed quickly. Sikes said farewell to Nancy and took

the boy by the hand, pausing a moment to show him, with
a menacing gesture, that the pistol was in his side pocket.

A cheerless morning greeted them outside. The wind was
blowing and rain lashed the streets. Dawn was still a faint
glimmer in the sky. Nobody was about yet. The lanes were silent
and empty.

Gradually London began to wake. A few country wagons were
slowly crawling towards the city and now and then a stage-coach,
covered with mud, rattled by. The public houses, with lamps
burning inside, were already open. Carts loaded with vegetables
and milkmaids with pails headed for market.

Sikes and Oliver reached London's famous meat market,
Smithfield. The place was full of noise. There were long lines of
pigs, cattle, oxen and sheep. Countrymen, butchers, cattle
drovers, boys, thieves, idlers and vagabonds all mingled together.
The sound of bleating sheep, grunting pigs, bells ringing and
market men shouting oaths filled the air. Everyone was crowding,
pushing, driving, whooping and yelling. Oliver was stunned by
the lively scene.

'Now, young 'un,' said Sikes. 'It's already seven o'clock. Don't
lag behind, lazy legs.'

Oliver broke into a kind of trot, half way between a fast walk
and a run, to keep up with Sikes. They crossed London and by
Hyde Park Corner they spied a cart.

'Give us a lift?' said Sikes. 'We're going west.'

'Jump up,' said the driver. 'Is that your boy?'

'Yes, he's my boy,' replied Sikes, putting his hand into the
pocket where the pistol lay

As milestone followed milestone and London was left behind,
Oliver wondered more and more where they were going. They
travelled all day and on into the evening. Soon night fell. It was
very dark. A damp mist rose from the marshy ground and it was
piercing cold too. Oliver sat huddled in a corner of the cart,
shivering with fear.

A few miles on, they left the cart and continued on foot.
Through the mist Oliver could see they were coming to a river.
Sikes suddenly turned down to the bank.

'The water!' thought Oliver, turning sick with fright. 'He's
going to murder me here.'

Then he saw that they stood in front of a solitary house. It was
ruined and decayed and, to all appearances, uninhabited. Sikes
opened the door and pulled Oliver in after him.

'Hello!' cried a voice.

'Don't make such a row,' hissed Sikes, bolting the door behind him.

Soon a man appeared. It was Toby Crackit, another of Sikes' robber friends. 'I'm glad to see you. You're so late I thought you weren't coming.'

'Never mind,' said Sikes. 'Give us something to eat while we're waiting. Oliver, sit by the fire. We'll be going out again soon.'

They ate quickly and then Oliver watched as Sikes and Toby prepared themselves. Toby produced a pair of pistols. 'The persuaders,' he muttered viciously.

They both drew large dark shawls around their chins and put on great-coats. Toby opened a cupboard and pulled out an iron crowbar.

'Come along, Oliver,' said Sikes. They opened the door and crept out into the night again. It was now intensely dark and the fog was much heavier than it had been earlier. The mist half froze in Oliver's hair.

They reached a small town and hurried through the main street. The place was deserted. Only an occasional light shone from a bedroom window. The barking of dogs broke the silence of the night. Oliver shivered as the church clock struck two o'clock.

After walking for a quarter of a mile they reached a house surrounded by a wall. Toby climbed it in a twinkling. Sikes hoisted Oliver to the top for his partner to help down the other side. Sikes followed them over. They crept cautiously towards the house.

And now for the first time, Oliver, stricken with terror, saw what they had come for: housebreaking, robbery and, perhaps, even murder. He sank to the ground.

'Get up,' whispered Sikes, drawing the pistol from his pocket. 'Get up, or I'll blow your brains out.'

'Let me go,' cried Oliver. 'Let me run away and die in the fields. I will never come near London again. Please don't make me steal.'

Sikes swore. 'Say another word, young 'un, and I'll crack your head open. Now come on. You'll do what we ask.'

Oliver fell silent and Sikes pulled him to the side of the house. Using a crowbar, he quickly opened the wooden shutter on a window. It was a tiny opening but large enough for Oliver to squeeze through.

'Now listen, you,' said Sikes, drawing a small lantern from his great-coat. 'I'm going to push you through that window. Take this

*'Now listen, you,' said Sikes, drawing a small lantern from his
great-coat. 'I'm going to push you through that window.'*

light and find your way into the hall and open up the front door for us.'

The window was quite high up. Toby bent down against the wall and Sikes stood on his back and lifted Oliver through the opening, feet first, and lowered him to the floor inside.

Oliver, more dead than alive with fear, opened the door of the room he found himself in. He had already decided that, whether he lived or died in the attempt, he would dart up the first stairs he found and warn the family.

But it wasn't to be. There was a sudden noise from the hall.

'Come back!' Sikes cried out aloud. 'Back! Back!'

Scared by the breaking of the dead silence, Oliver dropped his lantern and didn't know whether to go backwards or forwards. There was another shout and he saw two men running down a passage towards him.

There was a flash – a burst of smoke – a crash. Oliver staggered back.

Sikes fired his pistol at the men and grabbed Oliver's falling body and hauled him up and out of the window.

'They've shot him,' cried Sikes. 'Damnation, he's bleeding badly.'

Toby and Sikes, with Oliver over his shoulders, ran for their lives. They heard the front door of the house open and the sound of barking dogs giving chase.

Toby was soon far ahead and Sikes stopped by a ditch and shouted at him to come back and help with the boy. Toby stopped immediately. He knew he was still within range of his partner's pistol.

'It's all up,' cried Toby. 'Drop the boy and show 'em your heels.'

With that, Toby, preferring the chance of being shot by Sikes to the certainty of being taken by his enemies, turned tail and darted off at full speed.

Sikes clenched his teeth and took a look back. He could hear the pursuers but couldn't see them in the mist and darkness. He dropped Oliver to the ground and threw a cape over him and then ran off along the hedge.

He came to another hedge further on and, whirling his pistol high into the air, cleared it at a bound, and was gone.

## Chapter Seven

THE very next day in the town where Oliver was born,
Mr. Bumble, having returned from London, was on his way to the
workhouse. The scheming beadle had a plan. Mrs. Corney, the
workhouse matron, was having tea when he knocked on the door.

'Oh, come in,' she said sharply, angry at having her
tea interrupted. 'Some old pauper dying, I suppose. They always
die when I'm at meals.' She was surprised to see Mr. Bumble.
'Dear me, come in,' she said in a much sweeter tone.

It was snowing heavily outside and the beadle stopped on the
doormat to shake the flakes from his cocked hat.

'Hard weather,' said Mrs. Corney.

'Hard, indeed, ma'am,' said Mr. Bumble. 'I had to give away
twenty loaves of bread and some cheese this afternoon. And yet
them paupers are still not happy. Why, I gave half a pound of
potatoes to a man with a large family. All he could say was that
he'd still die in the streets from starvation, as it wasn't enough. So
I took them back. What an ungrateful wretch!'

'Ha! Ha!' laughed Mrs. Corney. 'What happened?'

'He went away and he did die in the streets. Now there's an
obstinate pauper for you!'

Mrs. Corney laughed again and offered Mr. Bumble a cup of
tea. The beadle quickly seated himself at the table and watched
Mrs. Corney closely as she poured him a cup and then sat down.

What was Mr. Bumble up to? The table was round and, moving
his chair little by little, the beadle inched himself closer to the
matron. Soon the two chairs touched. If the matron had moved
her chair away to the right she would have fallen into the fire, and,
if to the left, she would have dropped into Mr. Bumble's arms.
The matron, who had been widowed many a year, was trapped.

The beadle drank his tea, finished a piece of toast, whisked
some crumbs off his knee, wiped his lips and reached over to kiss
Mrs. Corney.

'Mr. Bumble!' cried the lady. 'I shall scream.' She had no
intention of screaming but Mr. Bumble's romantic plans were
interrupted by a knock at the door.

'If you please, mistress,' said a frail old woman. 'Old Sally is
dying. She's going fast.'

'What's that to me?' demanded the matron angrily. 'I can't
keep her alive, can I?'

The woman wasn't to be stopped. 'No, no, mistress. She says she has something to tell you, something you must hear before she dies. She'll never die until you come.'

Mrs. Corney muttered angrily again and, asking Mr. Bumble to wait for her return, went away with the woman.

Left alone, Mr. Bumble took the chance to see how wealthy the matron was. He opened a cupboard and counted the silver teaspoons, weighed the sugar tongs and inspected the milk pot to make sure it was made of real silver.

*        *        *        *        *

Mrs. Corney found Sally lying in bed at the top of the house. She was dozing and the light from a feeble fire threw a ghastly light over her shrivelled face.

As soon as Mrs. Corney entered the room, Sally awoke. 'Who's there?' she said, feebly raising herself.

'It's the matron,' said Mrs. Corney.

Sally clutched her by the arm. 'Listen to me,' said the dying woman. 'In this very room – in this very bed – I once nursed a pretty young girl who was brought into the workhouse. She gave birth to a boy and then died.'

'What about her?' said Mrs. Corney impatiently.

'I robbed her before she died,' said Sally, fading fast.

'Robbed her? What did you steal?'

'It was the only thing she had,' said Sally. 'It was gold, I tell you. Rich gold that might have saved her life.'

'Gold!' said the matron, interested at last. 'Who was the mother? When did this happen?'

'The boy grew so like his mother that I could never forget it when I saw his face. Poor girl. She was so young, such a gentle lamb. Wait! I have more to tell.'

'Be quick,' said Mrs. Corney, 'or it will be too late!'

Sally whispered. 'The mother told me before she died that one day her baby would be proud to learn of the name of its mother.'

'The boy's name?' demanded the matron.

'They called him Oliver,' replied Sally, 'the gold I stole was . . .'

'Yes. Yes – what?' cried Mrs. Corney. She bent eagerly over the woman to hear the answer. But Sally had spoken her last.

'Stone dead,' mumbled the matron.

It was then she noticed something in the dead woman's hand.

*        *        *        *        *

*'It was the only thing she had,' said Sally. 'It was*
*gold, I tell you. Rich gold that might have saved her life.'*

Mrs. Corney returned to Mr. Bumble in a very excited state. 'What distresses you?' asked the beadle.

'Oh, nothing,' replied Mrs. Corney. 'I'm just a foolish, excitable weak creature.'

'Not weak, ma'am?' answered Mr. Bumble, drawing his chair a little closer to her. 'Are you a weak creature, Mrs. Corney?'

'We are all weak creatures,' she sighed, as Mr. Bumble put his arm around her. He kissed her again.

They were silent for a few moments and then Mr. Bumble suddenly exclaimed. 'You know that the master of the workhouse is very ill, probably won't last another week.'

'Yes,' said Mrs. Corney, pretending not to understand what Mr. Bumble was getting at.

'His death will cause a vacancy. Oh, Mrs. Corney, what luck for us. We could become Master and Mistress of the workhouse together. We will marry. My dear Corney, we will marry.'

'Yes, yes,' sighed matron. 'Marry me as soon as you please. You are indeed a dove.'

She then sank into the dove's arms and he planted a kiss on her nose.

*        *        *        *        *

That evening a very happy beadle walked to see Mr. Sowerberry about a coffin for Sally. The coffin-maker and his wife were out but through a window he saw Oliver's old enemy Noah Claypole and the housekeeper Charlotte. They were kissing.

'What!' cried Mr. Bumble, bursting into the room. 'What are you doing?'

Charlotte uttered a scream and hid her face in an apron. Noah, who had been fed too much wine by the housekeeper, gazed at the beadle in drunken terror.

'I didn't mean to do it,' said Noah, blubbering. 'She's always kissing me whether I like it or not.'

'Silence,' ordered Mr. Bumble. 'Your master will hear of this. Kissing, indeed.' Mr. Bumble raised his hands in horror and strode with a lofty air out of the room.

## Chapter Eight

OLIVER lay motionless in the ditch where Sikes had dropped him, for a whole day. At last, as the evening mist began to roll along the ground like a cloud of smoke, he regained consciousness. He was so weak he could hardly raise himself into a sitting position.

Oliver knew that if he stayed where he was he would surely die. His arm, which had taken the blast of the shotgun, hung uselessly at his side. Trembling in every joint and exhausted by the cold, the boy painfully struggled to his feet. He was dizzy and staggered to and fro. But somehow he stumbled out of the ditch and onward.

He looked around and saw that there was a house close by. He summoned all his strength and moved closely towards it. As he drew near, Oliver realised he had seen the place before. It was the same house they had attempted to rob the evening before.

Oliver felt a terrible panic. For an instant he forgot his wound and thought of getting away. But he could hardly stand, let alone escape. He pushed open the garden gate and tottered across the lawn. He reached the door, knocked faintly and then sank down against it.

It was almost nightfall and inside the house Mr. Giles, the butler, was still boasting to the other servants how he had shot the robbers of the night before and sent them running. But now he was frightened again. He heard the knock and wondered whether the villains had returned.

Giles went to the door and slowly opened it. 'A boy!' he exclaimed, looking down at the sad figure of Oliver. He turned and called up the stairs to the owner of the house. 'Here's one of the thieves, ma'am. Wounded, miss. This is the one I shot.'

\*      \*      \*      \*      \*

Oliver was carried to a bed and a doctor called. Later that night the owner of the house, Mrs. Maylie, her young niece Rose and the doctor Mr. Losberne, were gathered around the bed of the sleeping boy.

'He's not in danger, is he?' asked Mrs. Maylie.

'I don't think so,' said Mr. Losberne.

Mrs. Maylie stared at poor Oliver. 'Can he really be one of the robbers?'

'And at such a young age,' said Rose, a pretty girl not yet seventeen years old. Her deep blue eyes shone with kindness.

The doctor sadly shook his head. 'Crime like death is not confined to the old and sick,' he said. 'The youngest and fairest are often its chosen victims.'

Rose looked at her aunt. 'But even if this boy has been wicked, think how young he is. Dear aunt, think of that before you let them drag him off to prison. Remember how I was an orphan, a homeless girl until you took pity on me and gave me a home and the love of a mother I never knew.'

Mrs. Maylie gave Rose a hug. 'I wouldn't harm a hair on his head. But what can we do to save him from the police? Giles sent for them this morning. The Bow Street Runners will be here soon.'

The doctor thought for a moment and pronounced: 'I have a plan.'

*          *          *          *          *

The next morning there was a knock at the door and a rough voice called out: 'Open the door . . . it's the officers of the law!'

Giles opened the door and the two men walked in as coolly as if they lived there. 'Tell your governor that Blathers and Duff is here, will you?' said Blathers, a stout fellow with half whiskers, a round face and sharp eyes.

The bumbling and pompous policemen were ushered into the presence of Mr. Losberne and Mrs. Maylie.

'From these here circumstances I doubt the robbers were local yokels,' said Blathers.

'Certainly not!' replied Duff, a red-headed man with a sinister turned-up nose.

'But from the small size of the window it's clear a boy was involved,' said Blathers, full of his own importance. 'Now what's this boy I've heard the servants mention?'

'Yes, who's this boy?' said Duff, not wanting to be left out of the detective work.

'Oh, nothing at all,' said Mr. Losberne. 'One of the frightened servants took it into his head that he had something to do with the robbery. But, of course, it's sheer nonsense.'

'We'll have to see the lad,' said Blathers.

'Yes, we'll have to see the lad,' echoed Duff.

Upstairs the officers were taken to see Oliver, still in a deep sleep and with his wounded arm in a sling.

'And why don't you think he was the robber's lad?'
said Blathers.

'Why not the robber's lad?' said Duff. 'He has been wounded,
after all.'

Mr. Losberne told the story he had planned to put the police off
the scent. 'The lad was accidentally shot by a gamekeeper's gun
while on a boyish prank. He came to our house for assistance.'

Blathers and Duff put their bumbling heads together in
a corner of the room and discussed the matter in whispers. 'If this
ain't the boy, then I reckon the robbery were done by Conkey
Chickweed and his lad,' mumbled Blathers.

'Ay, that'll be our man,' said Duff. 'Conkey's our man.'

The officers of the law turned to Mr. Losberne. 'We has
discussed the matter,' said Blathers, with the air of a man who has
just solved a crime. 'Our clever deductions, based on a superior
knowledge of the criminal kind, leads us to believe the robbery
was done by one Conkey Chickweed, a London villain well
known to us. We needn't trouble you any further.'

Blathers and Duff turned their suspicious but dull noses back
towards London.

*     *     *     *     *

The same day another man returned to London empty-handed.
It was Toby Crackit, who had run off after the robbery, leaving
Sikes and Oliver behind. Travelling by night and hiding by day,
he finally reached Fagin's grim den.

'Where's Sikes? Where's the boy?' screamed Fagin.

'The robbery failed,' said Toby. 'The boy was shot. The dogs
were after us. We all parted company and the youngster was left
in a ditch. Alive or dead, I know not.'

Fagin stamped furiously on the ground and gasped in fear. He
could feel the gallow's rope tightening around his neck! Uttering
a loud yell and tearing at his hair, he rushed out of the room and
into the street.

Avoiding the main streets, Fagin skulked through the back
alleys until he reached a dark haunt of thieves and criminals called
the Three Cripples Inn.

Fagin peered through the door, anxiously looking around. He
seemed to be looking for one particular man. He went in.

The room was dimly lit by two gas lights. Barred shutters and
closely drawn curtains prevented anyone from seeing in or out.
The ceiling was blackened by the lights and dense tobacco smoke

billowed into the air. Fagin looked eagerly at each face in the place. It was clear the man he wanted to see was not there.

Fagin spoke to the landlord. 'Will he be here tonight?'

'Monks, do you mean?' replied the landlord.

'Hush!' said Fagin sharply. 'Any business between me and him must remain a secret.'

'He's not here,' said the landlord, 'but he will be in a few minutes.'

'I can't wait,' hissed Fagin. 'Tell him I was here and that I must see him.'

The landlord promised to pass on the message and Fagin scurried out of the inn and headed for home again.

The streets were empty and a chill wind drove him back, trembling and shivering all the way. He had reached the corner of his own street and was fumbling in his pocket for the door key when a dark figure emerged from the shadows.

'Fagin!' whispered a voice close to his ear.

'Ah!' said the old man, quickly turning around. 'Is that you?'

'Yes,' said the figure who was dressed in a long black cloak. 'Where the devil have you been?'

'On your business,' replied Fagin, opening the door and urging the stranger quickly into the house. At the bottom of the stairs they stopped and a candle was lit. 'We can say what we've got to say here.'

They talked in whispers. It was clear from the conversation that the mysterious man was called Monks and that he was very angry with Fagin.

'Why didn't you keep Oliver here?' said Monks. 'Why risk him on a robbery? You could have turned him into a thief yourself. You know that's what I wanted. You've done it with other boys before. If you'd been patient you could have got Oliver arrested and convicted.'

'What good would that have done?' asked Fagin.

'It would have done me a lot of good,' said Monks. 'It was all I ever asked of you.'

Fagin fell quiet for a moment and then spoke again. 'The boy, with his angelic looks, could be worth hundreds of pounds to me . . . but I do remember that we have an agreement and both our interests should be considered.'

'What now?' demanded Monks sulkily.

'It wasn't easy trying to train the boy to be a thief,' answered Fagin. 'He's not like other boys I've had.'

'Curse the boy,' muttered Monks.

*'Fagin!' whispered a voice close to his ear.*
*'Ah!' said the old man, quickly turning around.*

'Oliver was not interested in thieving. What could I do? Look at the trouble I had when I first sent him out with Dodger and Charley. He got himself arrested.'

'That was not my doing,' said Monks.

'No,' replied Fagin eagerly. 'But if that had not happened you might never have clapped eyes on the boy and realised that he was the person you were searching for.'

Monks interrupted. 'I know I might never have found him but for his getting arrested.'

'And then I get him back for you with the help of Nancy,' said Fagin. 'And now she's beginning to like him.'

'Throttle the girl,' said Monks.

'We can't afford to do that just now, my dear,' replied Fagin, smiling. 'But one of these days I might be glad to. She could be trouble, that Nancy . . .'

Monks was getting impatient, his eyes nervously looking first over one shoulder and then the other, peering into the dark shadows.

Fagin continued. 'You want me to make Oliver a thief and I will if he's still alive,' he said. 'But if the worst comes to the worst and he's dead . . .'

A look of terror crossed the coward's eyes. 'It's no fault of mine if he is,' said Monks. 'If they shot him dead, it's nothing to do with me. I won't hang for Oliver.' Monks suddenly turned around. 'What's that?' he hissed.

'What?' asked Fagin. 'Where?'

'Yonder, I saw a shadow on the wall,' said Monks, terrified. 'The shadow of a woman in a cloak and bonnet.'

'You're just dreaming it,' said Fagin. 'We're alone here.'

'I'll swear I saw it!' trembled Monks. 'The shadow of a woman in a bonnet and cloak. She was bending forward when I first saw her. When I last spoke she darted away.'

Fagin insisted that there was nobody in the house except for Dodger and Charley and they were safely upstairs. Monks was finally convinced and with several grim laughs admitted that it must have been his imagination.

\*　　　\*　　　\*　　　\*　　　\*

In the street outside Fagin's house, Nancy wrapped her cloak closer to keep out the cold and hurried away.

## Chapter Nine

Oliver made a slow but happy recovery. Rose and Mrs. Maylie gave him much love and attention. He hadn't felt so happy since his days at Mr. Brownlow's house.

As soon as he was strong enough to speak, Oliver told them his sad story. They could hardly believe the list of evils and calamities which had happened to such a young boy.

'You are safe now,' said Rose, who had come to love Oliver like a brother.

'And I am so happy,' said Oliver. 'And yet I was thinking how ungrateful I am.'

'To whom?' asked Rose.

'To the kind gentleman, Mr. Brownlow, and Mrs. Bedwin who took so much care of me. If only they knew how happy I am now, they would be very pleased.'

'I'm sure they would,' said Rose. 'When you are well enough we will take you to see them.'

In a short time Oliver was fit enough to undertake the journey. They set off early one morning in Mrs. Maylie's coach. That evening they drove into the streets where Mr. Brownlow lived.

'There's the house. There! There!' shouted Oliver excitedly, pointing out of the coach window.

The coach stopped outside the house. Oliver was suddenly filled with disappointment. Outside the door was a large sign: 'TO LET'.

'Knock at the next door,' said Rose to the coachman. 'And find out what has happened to Mr. Brownlow.'

He returned a few minutes later. 'Mr. Brownlow and his housekeeper have sold up and gone to the West Indies,' he said.

It was bitter news for Oliver. Hopes of clearing his name with Mr. Brownlow had sustained him during all his hardship with Fagin and Sikes. Now they had gone away, still thinking he was an imposter and a thief. He felt the same way about Rose and Mrs. Maylie. It was almost too much for Oliver to bear. How would he ever prove to his friends that his story was true?

They drove back to Mrs. Maylie's home and over the next few weeks Oliver was happy that Rose's love for him hadn't changed.

Such happy days followed. Winter turned to spring and in the mornings Oliver would be afoot by six o'clock, roaming the fields and plundering the hedges for wild flowers. He hurried back to decorate the breakfast table with them.

During the day an old white-haired man in the village taught him to read and Rose gave him school lessons in his own room. In the afternoons he would work in the garden, tidying the flower beds. Rose and Mrs. Maylie were delighted with their new boy.

Oliver also had his secret places where he would go to be alone. There was a pretty churchyard nearby. He often sat there thinking of his mother, quietly crying to himself.

In the evenings Rose would sit at the piano and sing gentle songs. And when it was time to go to bed Oliver would happily go. Nights held no fear for him now. There were no nightmares of being sent to prison any more, nor black visions of Sikes and Fagin. But he still thought often of his friend Dick in the workhouse nursery.

\*     \*     \*     \*     \*

Oliver's happiness came to a sudden halt when one day Rose fell ill. She woke with a terrible fever. Mrs. Maylie was frightened she would die from it.

'Heaven would never let her die so young,' said Oliver. He dearly loved Rose.

'We must get help,' said Mrs. Maylie. 'You must run to the town to find Doctor Losberne. It's no more than four miles over the fields.'

Oliver set off without delay. He ran swiftly across the fields and down little lanes, now almost hidden by high corn in fields on either side. He stopped only for a few seconds to catch his breath now and again. Soon he reached the town.

Oliver was passing the entrance to an old inn when he suddenly bumped into a tall man. He was wrapped in a black cloak and his eyes stared at Oliver in surprise. It was the mysterious Mr. Monks.

'Hah!' cried Monks. 'What the devil's this!'

'I beg your pardon, sir,' said Oliver, frightened by the stranger. 'I was in a great hurry and I didn't see you coming.'

'Death!' muttered Monks to himself, glaring at the boy with his large dark eyes. 'Who would have thought it! To find the boy here! Grind him to ashes! He'll haunt me to my dying day.'

'I am sorry,' stammered Oliver, totally confused by the man and his strange looks. 'I hope I haven't hurt you.'

'Rot your bones!' murmured Monks in a horrible tone of voice. 'Curses on your head and black death on your heart, you imp. What are you doing here?'

Monks shook his fist at Oliver and gnashed his teeth. He took

a step towards the boy as if to grab him. But then he was
overcome by a strange fit and collapsed to the ground.

Oliver ran to a nearby house for help. He was convinced the
man, whoever he was, must be mad. Monks was carried away and
Oliver hurried on to complete his mission. He was greatly puzzled
at the man's behaviour but his thoughts for Rose were more
important at the moment.

\*          \*          \*          \*          \*

Rose grew rapidly worse and Mr. Losberne announced that
there was little hope for her. Oliver crept away to his secret place
in the churchyard and prayed for Rose. The sun shone brightly
and there was beauty all around him. Every tree was in leaf, every
flower in bloom, Oliver could not understand how the sun could
shine on so much beauty when he was so sad.

When he returned, Mrs. Maylie was sitting in the little parlour.
Oliver's heart sank because she had never left Rose's
bedside before.

'Rose has fallen into a deep sleep,' said Mrs. Maylie. 'It's in
God's hands whether she wakes again.'

Mrs. Maylie was very sad and tears fell from her unhappy eyes.
Oliver sat at her knees, his tiny hand holding hers. Shortly she
spoke again. 'Oliver, you know that I love you and Rose like my
own children,' she said. 'But I have never told you about Rose.
She is an orphan too.'

Oliver was very surprised. He had always thought Rose really
was Mrs. Maylie's niece.

'Just like you, she never knew her mother,' she continued.
'Somehow she came into the hands of a very poor family who
could hardly afford to keep her. I chanced on this family and took
pity on the little girl and brought her home with me. Rose has
been with me ever since. She is very dear to me now, just as
you are.'

Oliver's head sank into Mrs. Maylie's lap and he began to cry
for poor Rose.

\*          \*          \*          \*          \*

For days Rose's life hung in the balance. But one morning
Mr. Losberne came downstairs with the news they had all longed
to hear.

'She has woken from her fever,' he said. 'Rose will live!' Oliver

fell into his arms. He was happy again.

Oliver got up the next day with fresh heart. He picked wild flowers with all his old enthusiasm. The dew seemed to sparkle once more on the green grass. The sky was brighter and bluer than he had known it for days.

He worked hard again at his lessons, too. The little room where he studied was on the ground floor at the back of the house. Jessamine and honeysuckle crept around the window, which looked out onto meadows and trees.

One evening Oliver was poring over his books. It was hot and he had been working so hard that he fell asleep in his high-backed chair. Soon he was dreaming.

He could see he was in his own room and his books were lying on the table. Sweet smells from the plants outside filled his head. Suddenly the scene changed and the air became thick and heavy. He dreamed he was back in Fagin's house again. He could see the hideous old man pointing at him and whispering to another man.

'Hush, my dear,' he could hear Fagin saying. 'It is the boy. We have found him again.'

The other man in the dream replied: 'I couldn't mistake him. If you buried him fifty foot down I should know it was his grave, even if there wasn't a cross to mark it.'

The man seemed to speak with such dreadful hatred that Oliver woke with a start.

He screamed. It wasn't a dream. At the window, so close he could almost have touched him, was Fagin and another man peering into the room.

The terrifying figures were gone in a flash and Oliver cried for help.

Mr. Losberne and some of the servants rushed to Oliver's room.

'Fagin! Fagin!' cried Oliver, pointing to the woods. 'It was Fagin!'

Everyone gave chase and every ditch and hedge was searched. But it was in vain. Eventually they stood on top of a hill which gave a clear view in every direction. There wasn't a sign of anyone.

'It must have been a dream.' said Mr. Losberne.

'Oh, no sir,' said Oliver. 'I saw Fagin and another man as plainly as I see you now.'

'Who was the other man?'

'The very man I told you about, the strange man I met at the inn,' said Oliver.

The search went on until it was dark. Fagin and Monks had vanished into thin air.

*'Hush, my dear,' he could hear Fagin saying.*
*'It is the boy. We have found him again.'*

The matter was soon forgotten in the rush to organise a visit to London. Rose, Mrs. Maylie and Oliver were to stay a few days there in a hotel.

## Chapter Ten

MR. Bumble sat in the workhouse parlour. His eyes were fixed moodily on the empty fire grate. He was thinking about the changes that had happened in his life. The mighty cocked-hat of the beadle had gone. He now had a modest round hat. He was no longer a beadle.

Mr. Bumble had married Mrs. Corney and was now Master of the workhouse.

'Two months we've been married,' Mr. Bumble mumbled to himself. 'It seems a lifetime.' He sighed deeply. 'I sold myself for six teaspoons, a pair of sugar tongs, a silver milk pot and some second-hand furniture. I sold myself cheap, dirt cheap.'

'Cheap!' cried a shrill voice. 'You would have been expensive at any price.'

Mr. Bumble turned to find Mrs. Bumble at his ear.

'Are you going to sit snoring there all day?' she asked sharply.

'I'll sit here as long as I like, ma'am,' replied Mr. Bumble. 'And I was not snoring. Though I shall snore, sneeze, laugh or cry as the humour strikes. That is my right.'

'Your right!' sneered Mrs. Bumble.

'That's right, ma'am,' said Mr. Bumble. 'The right of a man is to command.'

'And what's the right of a woman, sir?' asked Mrs. Bumble.

'To obey, ma'am,' thundered Mr. Bumble, rising from his chair, putting his hat on and walking towards the door.

'We'll see who's to be obeyed here,' cried his angry wife, knocking his hat from his head with her hand and then showering him with blows. She leapt at him, scratched his face and finally sent him tumbling over a chair. 'Get up and take yourself away,' she screamed.

'Certainly, my dear,' cried a very alarmed Mr. Bumble, picking himself up and making a fast retreat to the door. 'I'm going . . . I'm going.'

The bully had met his match. Mr. Bumble crept out of the room. Unfortunately some minutes later he came to another room where some pauper woman were washing clothes.

'These women at least will continue to obey me,' said Mr. Bumble to himself. He walked into the room with a fierce and angry manner. 'What do you mean making all this noise, you hussies!' he cried.

He had hardly said the words when his eyes met his wife's. 'My dear,' he said. 'I didn't know you were in here.'

'And what are you doing here?' she snapped.

'I thought the women were talking too much to be doing any work,' he replied.

'What business is it of yours?' she replied. 'We don't need you interfering here. You are a great deal too fond of poking your nose into things that don't concern you.'

Mr. Bumble was horrified to see the pauper women giggling at him. Then Mrs. Bumble came at him with a bowl of soap suds. 'Be off with you or you'll get this,' she threatened.

What could Mr. Bumble do? He slunk out of the room as the women broke into cackles of laughter. He was humiliated. Once a powerful beadle, now he had sunk to the lowest depths of snubbed hen-peckery.

'All in two months,' said Mr. Bumble dismally. 'Two months ago I was on my own and everybody else's master . . . and now!'

It was too much. Mr. Bumble boxed the ears of a boy who opened the workhouse gate for him and walked out into the street. He felt thirsty and walked to an inn. The place was deserted except for one other customer.

The man, seated in a corner, was tall and dark. He was wearing a long black coat. The mysterious stranger eyed Mr. Bumble as he came in. 'I have seen you before, I think,' said the man. 'You were the beadle in this town once, weren't you?'

'I was,' said Mr. Bumble, surprised that the man knew him. 'I am now Master of the workhouse.'

The stranger looked closely into Mr. Bumbles eyes. 'I know you well,' said the man. 'And do you still have an eye to earning an extra pound or two when you can?'

Mr. Bumble was quite taken aback. But the talk of money was

enough to tempt him to talk further. 'Officers of the parish are
not so well paid that they would refuse a little extra,' he said.

The stranger smiled and nodded his head, as if to say he had
not mistaken his man. Then he rang the bell. 'Fill his glass,
landlord,' he said. 'I'm sure he likes it strong.'

'Not too strong,' said Mr. Bumble, with a delicate cough.

The landlord returned and Mr. Bumble's first gulp brought
tears into his eyes.

'Now listen to me,' said the stranger. 'I came to this town to
find you. By chance you walk into the very room where I am
sitting. I want some information from you. I don't ask it
for nothing.'

He pushed two gold sovereigns across the table to Mr. Bumble,
who examined the coins to make sure they were genuine. Then he
quickly dropped them into his waistcoat pocket.

'You don't know me,' said the man, 'and I advise you not to try
and find out. But for your two sovereigns I'd like you to cast your
mind back . . . let me see . . . ten or eleven years ago.'

'It's a long time,' said Mr. Bumble. 'But, yes, I can remember
the time.'

'The scene is the workhouse,' continued the mysterious stranger.
'Good!'

'And the time, night.'

'Yes,' said Mr. Bumble.

'A boy was born there,' said the man.

'A great many boys and girls were born there,' said
Mr. Bumble, shaking his head.

'Young devils all,' said the stranger. 'I speak of a pale-faced
boy who was later sent to work at the coffin-maker's.'

'Why, you mean Oliver!' cried Mr. Bumble excitedly. 'Young
Twist. Of course I remember him. There wasn't a more
obstinate rascal . . .'

The stranger interrupted. 'It's not him I want to hear about.
I've heard too much of him already. It's a woman, the old hag
Sally that nursed his mother, I want to hear about. Where is she?'

'She died last winter,' replied Mr. Bumble.

The man stared at Mr. Bumble for some time and then lost
himself in thought. It seemed as though the man didn't know
whether to be pleased or disappointed with the information. Then
he stood up as if to leave. 'It is no matter in any case,' he said,
walking towards the door.

But Mr. Bumble was cunning enough. He saw an opportunity
for earning some more money. He well remembered the night he

had proposed marriage to Mrs. Corney and how she had been called to the death-bed of old Sally, who had once nursed Oliver.

'My wife was with the nurse the night she died,' said Mr. Bumble quickly. 'She might be able to throw some light on the matter.'

The man stopped suddenly. 'How can I find her?' he said, with fear in his eyes.

'I can arrange a meeting,' said Mr. Bumble.

'When?' cried the stranger urgently.

'Tomorrow evening?' inquired Mr. Bumble.

'I'll meet you at nine o'clock,' said the stranger. He produced a scrap of paper and wrote down the address of an old mill. 'Bring your wife to me there. And I needn't tell you to be secret about all of this. It's in your interest.'

With those words, they walked to the door and, once into the street, said farewell and went their separate ways.

But Mr. Bumble looked at the address and saw that it contained no name. He stopped and seeing the man had not gone far, raced after him.

'Who's that?' the man said in alarm, quickly turning round as Mr. Bumble touched his arm. 'Are you following me?'

'Only to ask a question,' said the pursuer, pointing to the scrap of paper. 'What name am I to ask for?'

'Monks,' whispered the stranger and strode hastily into the night.

\*       \*       \*       \*       \*

The next evening Mr. and Mrs. Bumble turned out of the town's main street and walked towards a group of ruined houses by a river. The summer sky was overcast and the clouds threatened a violent thunder storm. They were both dressed in shabby old clothes. They didn't want anybody to recognise them.

The people who lived in the marshy area were desperate ruffians; they lived by crime. The houses were a collection of hovels built a few yards from the bank. A few leaky boats were drawn up on the mud.

At the heart of the area stood a large mill, which had long since gone to ruin. Rats and the weather had weakened the foundations and already part of the building had sunk into the river. The rest of the wooden construction leaned dangerously over the dark stream.

The first peal of thunder roared down from the sky,

quickly followed by a torrent of rain.

'The place should be here somewhere,' said Mr. Bumble, examining his scrap of paper.

'Hello there!' cried a voice from above.

Mr. Bumble saw a man peering down from a window on the second storey of the mill. 'Stand where you are. I'll be down in a minute,' shouted Monks.

Mr. Bumble was frightened and might have scampered off home but for the arrival of Monks at the door.

'Come in quickly!' he said, stamping his foot impatiently. 'Don't keep me waiting.'

They followed him into the shadowy mill and Monks turned to gaze at Mrs. Bumble. 'This is the woman, is it?' he demanded.

'It is,' said Mr. Bumble.

'You can keep secrets, can you ma'am?' Monks asked.

'You don't think women can keep secrets?' asked Mrs. Bumble angrily.

'You will keep secret about what happens tonight,' threatened Monks. 'I know you will. Anyone who knows a secret which might hang them will keep it quiet. Do you understand me?'

'No,' said Mrs. Bumble, her face going slightly pale.

'Of course, you don't,' sneered Monks. 'How could you know?'

Monks beckoned his companions to follow him again. He was about to climb up a steep ladder to a room above when a bright flash of lightning streamed across the mill and a peal of thunder followed. The whole building shook.

Monks shrank back. 'Hear it! Rolling and crashing as if it echoed through a thousand caverns where devils are hiding. I hate the sound.'

Mr. Bumble saw Monks' face. It was distorted and ghostly white. They climbed the ladder and found themselves in a dark room, lit only by the fading evening light trickling through a rotten window. Monks quickly closed the window and lit a lamp. It shed the dimmest light on an old table surrounded by three chairs.

'Now,' said Monks, when they had all sat down. 'The sooner we get this business over with, the better. Were you with the nurse Sally when she died and did she tell you something?'

'Yes,' said Mrs. Bumble. 'She told me something about the mother of Oliver Twist.'

'Then the first question is,' said Monks, 'what did she tell you?'

'That's not the first question,' said the woman. 'The first is how

*The first peal of thunder roared down from
the sky, quickly followed by a torrent of rain.*

much will you pay for the information?'

Monks was angry. 'Who the devil can tell without knowing what it is.'

'Nobody better than you if I understand right,' said Mrs. Bumble. 'What's it worth to you?'

'It may be nothing. It may be twenty pounds,' replied Monks. 'Speak out and let me know.'

Mrs. Bumble replied instantly. 'Make it twenty-five pounds and I'll tell you all I know.'

'That is a large sum for a secret which may be nothing and has been lying dead for years,' said Monks. 'What if I am paying for nothing?'

'You can easily take it away again if it's not worth it,' said the scheming woman. 'I am but a woman, alone and unprotected.'

Her gallant husband interrupted. 'Not alone, my dear, nor unprotected. I am here, my dear.'

'You are a fool,' said Mrs. Bumble, 'and you'd better hold your tongue.'

Mr. Bumble sat back in silence and watched as Monks produced a wallet and drew out twenty-five pounds. He laid it on the table and pushed it over to the woman. 'Now,' he said, as thunder shook the building again, 'let's hear your story.'

The faces of the three nearly touched as the two men leant over the table to hear Mrs. Bumble's whisper. 'Sally spoke of a young woman who gave birth to a son who was called Oliver Twist. The woman died and Sally said she robbed her of something . . . something gold . . .'

Monks interrupted with desperate eagerness. 'Did she sell it? Who to? Where? When?'

'That was the last thing she said,' answered Mrs. Bumble. 'She just fell back and died.'

'Without saying another word?' cried Monks furiously. 'It's a lie. She must have said more. I'll tear the life out of both of you if you don't tell me what it was.'

'She didn't utter another word,' said Mrs. Bumble. 'But . . . but as she died she clasped my dress quite violently with one hand. In that hand I found a piece of paper . . .'

'What was it? What did it contain?' said Monks.

'It was a pawnbroker's ticket,' said the woman. 'A pawnbroker had given Sally some money in exchange for something. She obviously kept the ticket in case she wanted to buy it back one day.'

'What did you do with the ticket?' said Monks very impatiently.

'I went to the pawnbroker and exchanged the ticket for some items,' said Mrs. Bumble. 'I wasn't stealing, of course. I just felt that something might come of it one day.'

'And so it has,' said Monks excitedly. 'Where are the things now?'

'Here,' replied the woman as though she was relieved to be rid of them. She hastily threw a small bag on the table.

Monks pounced on it and tore the bag open with trembling hands. It contained a little gold locket, in which there were two locks of hair, and a plain gold wedding ring.

'It has the word 'Agnes' engraved on the inside,' said Mrs. Bumble, 'and then follows the date. You'll see it is within a year of Oliver's birth.'

'And this is all?' asked Monks, keenly examining the items.

'All,' replied the woman.

Mr. Bumble drew a breath, glad to hear the story was over without Monks asking for his twenty-five pounds back. At last he took out a handkerchief and wiped off the perspiration which had been trickling down his face.

Mrs. Bumble was still troubled. 'What are you going to do with the jewels? Can they be used by the police or anyone against me?'

'Never!' answered Monks. 'Not against me either. See here! But don't move a step or your life's not worth a halfpenny.'

With those words he pushed the table aside to reveal an iron ring set into the floorboards. He pulled at it and up came a large trap door.

'Look down,' said Monks, lowering the lantern into the black hole. 'And don't worry now. I could have dropped you both down the pit at any time if I'd felt like it.'

Both Mr. Bumble and his wife drew near to the brink and peered down. A long way below the river, swollen by the heavy rain, rushed beneath the building. The waters roared through the green and slimy foundations of the old mill.

'If I flung a man's body down there, where would it be tomorrow morning?' asked Monks, swinging the lantern to and fro in the evil-smelling pit.

Mr. Bumble shivered. 'Twelve miles down the river and cut to pieces, no doubt.'

Monks put the locket and the ring back into its bag and tied a lead weight around it. Then he dropped it through the trapdoor. It fell straight and true into the foaming waters.

'There!' said Monks, closing the trapdoor. 'They say that if the sea gives up its dead it will keep its gold and silver. So the deed is

done. We have nothing more to say to each other and we must go!'

'By all means,' said Mr. Bumble, only too keen to get out of the haunted mill.

When they got outside again Monks threatened them once more. 'Keep your silence or your lives could be in danger. The hangman's rope could be waiting for you both!'

Both Bumbles shivered again and quickly vanished into the darkness.

## Chapter Eleven

SIKES had moved to new lodgings since his return to London from the scene of the robbery. He now lived close to the River Thames and the damp had given him a nasty chill.

'What time of night is it?' he growled, awakening from a feverish sleep. He was lying in bed wrapped in a white dressing gown and wearing a dirty nightcap. A week's growth of beard covered his jaw. His dog Bull's-eye sat beside the bed, eyeing his master and growling at any noise in the street outside.

'Not long gone seven o'clock,' replied Nancy, busy by the window mending one of Sikes' jackets. 'How do you feel tonight, Bill?'

'As weak as water,' said Sikes. 'Here. Lend us a hand and get us off this bed.'

Illness had not improved Sikes' temper. As the girl lifted him up and helped him to a chair, he muttered curses and struck her a couple of times.

'You'd be more thoughtful if you thought of all the long nights I've looked after you,' said Nancy. 'I've nursed you like a child.'

'Whining again, eh?' said Sikes. 'If you can't do anything better than that you should clear out altogether. D'yer hear me?'

'I hear you,' said Nancy sulkily.

At that moment Fagin, Dodger and Charley arrived to visit Sikes. 'What's the matter here?' said Fagin.

'Nothing,' snarled Sikes. 'What evil wind has blown you here?'

'No evil wind, my dear,' replied Fagin. 'I've brought you something good. Dodger, my dear, open the bundle and give Bill the little trifles we all spent our money on this morning.'

The Dodger untied the bundle and put various articles on a table. Then he began to list all they had brought. 'Rabbit pie,' said Dodger. 'Such delicate creatures with such tender limbs . . . bones that melt in your mouth. Half a pound of tea so strong it'll blow the lid off the tea-pot, a pound and a half of sugar, two loaves of bread and some double Gloucester cheese, the richest sort you ever tasted.'

Dodger completed the feast by producing from one of his huge pockets a bottle of wine. 'You'll be all right now, Bill,' said Fagin.

'I'd say thank you,' said Sikes. 'But why have you not been to see me for so long. You take less notice of me than you would that there dog.'

Bull's-eye growled viciously and retreated under the bed.

'What have you got to say for yourself, you withered old thief?' said Sikes.

'I have been away from London on business, my dear. Just checking where our dear Oliver is,' replied Fagin. 'Don't be bad-tempered, my dear.'

'Business!' sneered Sikes. 'The boy will be the death of you.' Then Sikes changed the subject. 'I must have some money from you tonight. I want to go out.'

'I haven't a penny on me!' said Fagin.

'Then you must have lots at home,' snapped Sikes.

'Lots!' cried Fagin, holding his hands up in horror. 'I am but a poor man.'

'I don't know how much you've got but I know it takes you a long time to count it. Be gone with you and take Nancy . . . she'll bring the money back.'

*     *     *     *     *

It was late at night when Fagin and Nancy reached their destination. They hurried upstairs and the old man pulled a key from his pocket.

'It's just the key of a little cupboard where I keep a few things for the boys,' Fagin told Nancy. 'I never lock up my money because I've got so little my dear – ha! ha! ha! – none to lock up at

all. It's a poor trade I'm in.'

Fagin had just unlocked the cupboard when there was a knock at the front door.

'Bah!' said Fagin. 'It's the man I expected. Now Nancy, you stay here while I go and talk with him. He won't stop long.'

The old man picked up a candle and went downstairs to open the door. It was Monks.

'Any news?' asked Fagin.

'Plenty,' said Monks.

'Good news?'

'Not bad at all,' said Monks, with a smile. 'Now I must have a word with you in private.'

Nancy heard the two men come upstairs and then continue on to a room in the top storey of the house. Before the sound of their footsteps had stopped creaking on the floorboards, she had slipped off her shoes and crept silently upstairs. She reached a door and began listening with breathless interest to the whispers coming from the other side. Just before Fagin and Monks' conversation ended, Nancy flitted downstairs again.

Monks left immediately and Fagin returned to the tiresome task of finding Sikes some money. When he got back to the room Nancy was innocently adjusting her shawl and bonnet.

'Why, Nancy,' exclaimed Fagin. 'How pale you have suddenly turned.'

'Pale?' echoed Nancy.

'Yes, my dear. What have you been doing?'

'Nothing that I know of, except sitting in this room,' said Nancy. 'Now, come on, get the money and let me get back to Bill.'

With a sigh at every penny, Fagin counted out the amount into Nancy's hand and then bid her goodnight.

Once into the street Nancy sat down on a doorstep. She seemed completely bewildered. Suddenly she got up again and began running in the opposite direction, away from Sikes' place. She ran until she was exhausted and then stopped.

She was in a terrible state. She wrung her hands and burst into tears. What she had overheard had left her totally confused. But little by little she saw what she had to do. She turned back and hurried home to Sikes.

Sikes didn't see how agitated she was and, with a growl of satisfaction at receiving the money, fell asleep.

The next morning Sikes left the house and spent a whole day

'Not bad at all,' said Monks, with a smile. 'Now I must have
a word with you in private.'

getting very drunk with his new-found wealth. As the day progressed Nancy became more and more excited and anxious.

Sikes returned home and was busy drinking more gin in bed when he noticed Nancy's strange looks.

'You look like a corpse come to life again,' he said. 'What's the matter?'

'Matter?' replied the girl. 'Nothing.'

Sikes grabbed her arm and shook her roughly. 'What are you thinking about?'

'Nothing,' said Nancy with a shiver.

Sikes was very suspicious. 'I tell you what it is. You're not turning against me, are you, you're not going to . . . no, you wouldn't do that.'

'Do what?' said Nancy.

'No, you wouldn't go to the police. No. There ain't a stauncher-hearted girl than you, or I'd have cut your throat months ago. No, I know what it is. You've got the fever coming on.'

Sikes seemed satisfied with his own explanation and called for his medicine. Nancy jumped up quickly and went to a cupboard. With her back turned to Sikes, she poured some medicine from a green bottle into a glass.

Sikes drank it. 'Now, come and sit beside me,' he said with a threatening look in his eyes.

The girl obeyed and Sikes locked her hand in his. As he lay there, his eyes closed and then opened again. He shifted about restlessly and dozed off again. He kept waking up, often springing up with a look of terror in his eyes and gazing strangely. But soon the grasp of his hand relaxed and he lay quiet. He was in a deep and heavy sleep.

'The sleeping drug has worked at last,' said Nancy to herself as she rose from the bed. 'I may be too late, even now,'

Nancy got ready to go out, all the time looking fearfully around in case Sikes should suddenly awake. Then, stooping softly over the bed, she kissed the robber on the lips and hurried from the house.

Nancy ran all the way. She tore along the pavements, elbowing pedestrians out of the way and darting under horses' heads.

'The woman is mad,' said people, turning to see her rushing away.

When she reached the more wealthy part of town, the streets were almost deserted. Her destination was a small family hotel on the edge of London's famous Hyde Park. The clock struck eleven o'clock as she reached the entrance steps.

Inside she was met by a porter. 'Now, young woman, what do you want here?'

'I want to speak to a lady who is in this house,' said Nancy, breathlessly. 'A Miss Rose Maylie.'

## Chapter Twelve

NANCY'S life had been wasted by a life of crime in the worst areas and dens of London. Fagin had seen to that. Yet even the evil old man hadn't destroyed Nancy's gentle nature, nor her pride. She felt a deep sense of shame as the porter led her to Rose's door. She was more used to the company of thieves and ruffians, the outcasts of low haunts and the dregs of the jails. The thought of meeting a real lady frightened her.

Nancy was led into Rose's room. She curtsied and said: 'You are Rose Maylie?'

'Yes,' replied Rose. 'Tell me why you wanted to see me. I will be happy to help you if I can.'

The kind tone of Rose's voice and her gentle manner took Nancy by surprise and tears crept into her eyes.

'Sit down,' said Rose. 'You mustn't distress yourself. Now tell me what you want to say.'

Nancy hesitated for a moment, almost too terrified to speak. But then she began. 'I am about to put my life and the lives of others in your hands,' she said. 'I am the girl who dragged little Oliver back to Fagin on the night he left Mr. Brownlow's house.'

'You!' exclaimed Rose. 'You took him the night he was taking some books back for Mr. Brownlow?'

'Yes, lady,' replied Nancy. 'I am the infamous creature you have doubtless heard about. The alley and the gutter have been my world, as they will be my death bed.'

'Poor girl,' said Rose. 'It breaks my heart to hear it.'

'Bless you for your kindness,' said Nancy, her tears falling

freely. 'But I must be quick. I have run away from people who would surely murder me if they knew I was here. I have come to tell you something I have overheard. Do you know a man called Monks?'

Rose looked puzzled. 'No, I know nobody of that name.'

'He knows you,' said Nancy quickly. 'And he knows you are here because I heard him say your name and this hotel. He'd followed you from your house in the country.'

'No, I never heard his name before,' said Rose.

'Then he is using a false name,' said Nancy. 'I suspected as much a long time ago. But I'll go on. I overheard a conversation between this man called Monks and Fagin. I discovered then that Monks had been searching for Oliver for some time and had by chance seen him on the day that the boy had gone out pick-pocketing with two of our lads.'

Rose interrupted. 'That was the day Oliver was arrested and taken before the magistrate?'

'Yes,' said Nancy. 'I couldn't understand why Monks had been searching for Oliver but I heard Fagin talk of a bargain he'd made with Monks. If Fagin could turn Oliver into a thief then Monks would pay a lot of money.'

Rose was astonished. 'Why ever did he want to do that? Did you hear more?'

'Not that night,' said Nancy. 'Monks caught sight of my shadow and I had to escape quickly. But last night Monks came to see Fagin again.'

'And what happened?' Rose asked eagerly.

'I listened at the door and I heard Monks quite clearly. He said: "So the only evidence of the boy's identity lies at the bottom of the mill stream and the old hag that stole 'em from his mother is rotting in her coffin".'

Rose was astounded. 'What could all this mean?'

'After that,' said Nancy, 'they began to laugh and talk about how clever they had been. Monks raved on about how he had got Oliver's money safely now. And he mentioned a will . . . his father's will.'

'It's very strange,' said Rose. 'What is this all about?'

'There's more,' said Nancy. 'I heard Monks say that he would gladly kill the boy if he could do it without putting his own neck in danger. He said that wasn't possible at the moment, but threatened that if Oliver ever found out the true story of his birth and the identity of his mother and father he might have to.'

Rose shuddered with fright at the thought of someone wanting to kill Oliver. 'Go on,' she said.

'Monks told Fagin that he would keep a regular watch on Oliver for the rest of his life to make sure he didn't discover his past. Then the very last thing I heard him say was the most important. Monks said: "Fagin, you have done bad things in your life, but nothing as bad as I will do to my young brother, Oliver, if he finds out the truth".'

'His brother!' exclaimed Rose.

'Those were Monks' words,' said Nancy, who was now becoming very anxious. 'And more, he said that heaven or the devil must have contrived that Oliver should come into your hands. For how many thousands of pounds would you not give to know who Oliver is. Now I must get back.'

'Back?' said Rose, surprised. 'Why do you want to go back? I can get help immediately and we'll soon find a safe place.'

'I have to go back,' said Nancy. 'There is a man, the most desperate of all the people I have told you about. I can't leave him, not even to be saved from the life I lead. However bad he is, I still love him.'

Rose did not understand. 'You have come here to help little Oliver at so great risk to yourself and you want to return. Stay with me and I will save you.'

'Dear lady,' said Nancy. 'You are the kindest lady I have ever met. But it is too late to save me. And I cannot leave him. I cannot leave him now. He is the cruellest man but I would not cause his death.'

Rose realised she could not persuade Nancy to stay. 'How can this mystery about Oliver be investigated if you go?'

'There must be a gentleman you know who can advise you,' said Nancy. 'But he must keep the matter a secret.'

'Where can I find you again?' asked Rose. 'I promise I won't try to seek out Fagin and the other people you mentioned.'

'I will tell you if you promise to keep my secret and come alone or with just one other person,' said Nancy.

'I promise you solemnly,' said Rose.

'Every Sunday night after midnight I will walk on London Bridge. If I am alive that's where I will be.'

Rose made a last attempt to persuade Nancy to stay but it was of no use.

'God bless you, lady,' said Nancy as she left. 'And may he send you as much happiness on your head as I have brought shame on mine.'

\*      \*      \*      \*      \*

Rose didn't know what to do. Nancy's words had touched her heart. She didn't want to do anything which might get the girl into trouble.

Rose was still puzzling over the problem the following morning when Oliver, who had been walking in the streets with one of the servants for a bodyguard, burst into the room. He was in a breathless and very excited state.

'I've seen him! I've seen him!' cried Oliver. 'Now you will know that I have told you the truth.'

'I have never thought you told us anything but the truth,' said Rose. 'Who have you seen?'

'Mr. Brownlow! I saw him getting out of a coach,' said Oliver. 'I was trembling so much I couldn't speak to him. But the servant asked the coach driver where he lived. I have his address!'

'Quick!' said Rose. 'We must go there without a minute's delay.'

Oliver needed no encouragement. Within minutes a coach carried them to the address. Rose left Oliver in the coach and soon found herself in the presence of Mr. Brownlow.

'I expect I shall surprise you very much,' said Rose. 'But you once showed great kindness to a dear friend of mine, a person I am sure you will be pleased to hear of again.'

'Indeed?' said Mr. Brownlow curiously.

'His name is Oliver Twist,' Rose announced.

Mr. Brownlow was astonished. 'Oliver? You have news of Oliver?'

'I have indeed,' said Rose happily.

Mr. Brownlow moved his chair closer to hers and looked anxiously into her eyes. 'I once had an unfavourable opinion of that boy. Yet I have been on business abroad and since then I have discovered certain things which made me believe that perhaps he wasn't a thief. I did everything in my power to find him again but to no avail. Tell me your news.'

'Oliver is a child of gentle nature and warm heart,' said Rose. 'He was never a thief.'

Rose told Mr. Brownlow the story of what had happened to Oliver since leaving his house.

'Thank God,' said Mr. Brownlow. 'This is a great happiness to me. But you have not told me where he is now.'

'He is waiting in the coach outside,' said Rose.

'Here?' cried the old gentleman, getting up and hurrying down the stairs. In a moment he was at the coach door. Oliver jumped into his welcoming arms and a tear came to Mr. Brownlow's eyes.

*Mr. Brownlow was astonished. 'Oliver? You have news of Oliver?'*

The reunited pair walked back into the house and
Mr. Brownlow immediately rang for Mrs. Bedwin.

The old housekeeper answered his call and soon stood at the
door waiting for her orders.

'Why, you get blinder every day,' said Mr. Brownlow. 'Put on
your glasses and see if there's not someone here you have long
waited to see again.'

The lady began to rummage in her pocket for her spectacles.
But Oliver couldn't wait. He dashed across the room and threw
his arms around her.

'God be good to me!' she cried, embracing Oliver. 'It is my
innocent boy returned.'

'My dear old nurse!' sobbed Oliver.

'I knew he would come back,' said Mrs. Bedwin. 'How well he
looks, and how like a gentleman's son he is dressed again. The
same sweet face, but not so pale; the same soft eyes, but not so sad.'

Mr. Brownlow and Rose left Oliver with Mrs. Bedwin and
moved into another room. There Rose decided that
Mr. Brownlow was the man she must trust with Nancy's secrets.

\*       \*       \*       \*       \*

It was late when Oliver and Rose returned to the hotel with
Mr. Brownlow. He quickly called a conference to plan what they
had to do. But first they put Oliver to bed. He was tired after the
day's excitement and everyone agreed that it was best not to
reveal to him yet what they knew.

'We must proceed gently and with great care,' said
Mr. Brownlow. 'If we are to discover who Oliver's parents are
and recover his inheritance – if that story be true – we must be
clever.'

'How will we go about it?' asked Rose.

'It is quite clear,' began Mr. Brownlow, 'that we shall have
extreme difficulty in getting to the bottom of the mystery unless
we can bring this man Monks, whoever he is, to his knees. We can
only do that by catching him when Fagin and his gang are not
around.'

'That will be difficult,' Rose pointed out.

'We must see Nancy to ask whether she can lead us to the man,'
said Mr. Brownlow. 'It now being Tuesday we will have to wait
until Sunday night. I suggest we keep perfectly quiet until then
and keep all these matters secret from Oliver himself.'

Rose agreed to the plan and was about to go to her room when

Mr. Brownlow began speaking again. It was as though he spoke in riddles.

'It might seem odd that I wasn't here when you first visited my home with Oliver. As you know I was in the West Indies. I was there for a purpose in connection with the mystery surrounding Oliver.'

Rose looked on, surprised at the revelation. 'Why did you go there, sir?' she asked.

'I can make no answers at the moment,' he answered. 'Please don't ask me anything now because I don't want to raise anybody's hopes, in case they come to nought.'

Rose was distinctly puzzled.

## Chapter Thirteen

O N the very evening of Oliver's reunion with Mr. Brownlow, two more of his acquaintances were walking towards London. One was a young woman, a heavy bundle of baggage strapped to her back. The other was a red-nosed man with just a small bag dangling from a stick over his shoulder. His load was so much lighter that he moved a half dozen paces ahead of his companion.

'Come on, can't yer? What a lazybones you are, Charlotte,' said the man. It was Oliver's old enemy from the coffin shop, Noah Claypole.

'Is it much farther?' asked Charlotte.

'We're as good as there,' said Noah. 'Look there! Just ahead are the lights of London.'

'They're a good two miles off,' said Charlotte, breathing heavily under her load.

'Never mind that,' snapped Noah. 'Two miles or twenty, you better hurry up or I'll give you a kick.'

'Can't we stop at the nearest public house for the night?'

pleaded Charlotte.

'A fine thing that would be, wouldn't it,' jeered Noah. 'If we stopped at the first public house outside town, old Sowerberry might find us and take us back in handcuffs. No, we will lose ourselves in the narrowest streets we can find. If I wasn't here to think for you, Charlotte, you'd have been locked up in prison long ago.'

'I know I ain't as cunning as you, Noah,' replied Charlotte. 'But don't forget if I was locked up you would be too.'

'You took the money from Sowerberry's till,' Noah reminded Charlotte.

'I took it for you,' answered Charlotte.

'Did I keep it?' asked Noah.

'No,' said Charlotte. 'You trusted me to carry it for you. It's in my baggage.'

Indeed Noah, far from trusting his lady, had made sure Charlotte carried the stolen money. If they were arrested the money would be found on her and he could claim innocence.

They walked on into the night. Soon they were lurking in the darkest streets of London. Noah spotted a public house. 'That's good enough for the night,' said Noah, looking up at the sign outside the building. It was the Three Cripples Inn.

They entered the dreary building.

*     *     *     *     *

Later Noah and Charlotte tucked into a meal of cold meat and beer in a small back room of the inn. They began discussing their new life in London. They were so busy talking they didn't notice an evil old gentleman peering at them through a tiny glass window and listening to the conversation.

'I mean to be a gentleman,' said Noah. 'No more jolly coffins for me. And if you like, you shall be a lady.'

'I should like that,' replied Charlotte. 'But we need money and we can't steal from tills every day.

'Tills, be blowed,' said Noah, kicking out his legs boastfully. 'There's more things than tills to be emptied . . . I could pick pockets, rob houses, mail coaches and banks!'

'But you can't do all that,' said Charlotte.

'I shall find someone to help us,' said Noah, getting bolder with each sip of beer. 'I fancy myself as a leader of a gang.'

At that moment the eavesdropper appeared in the room. It was Fagin. He made a low bow and sat down at Noah's table and

*At that moment the eavesdropper appeared in the room.*

called for a drink.

'A pleasant night, sir,' said Fagin, rubbing his hands. 'From the country, I see, sir.'

'How do you know that?' said Noah.

'The dust on yer boots,' said Fagin. 'There ain't that much dust in London.'

'Yer a sharp fellow,' said Noah.

'You need to be sharp in this town,' replied Fagin, his voice shrinking into a low whisper. 'And that's the truth. Know what I mean?' Fagin tapped his nose with a finger and Noah, knowingly, did the same.

Fagin continued. 'I couldn't help but overhear your conversation and I think I can help you. I'm in your kind of business. What sort of work would you like to do?'

Noah trembled a little. The snivelling coward could boast of picking pockets and robbing banks but the thought of actually doing those jobs frightened him.

'Er, I think I should do something not too trying for my strength,' said Noah. 'Something not very dangerous.'

'What do you think of old ladies,' said Fagin. 'There's a great deal of money to be made from snatching their bags and parcels and then running around the corner.'

'Don't they cry out a lot and scratch sometimes?' asked Noah. 'Isn't there something else I could do?'

'What about children?' said Fagin. 'The young children on errands for their mothers with sixpence in their hands. They're easy to knock down and rob.'

'Ha! Ha!' laughed Noah. 'That's the very thing for me.'

Fagin laughed with him for a while and then asked: 'How about a bit of spying too? I have a friend who very much needs someone to do some spying for him.'

Noah thought for a moment. 'Yes, I think I could turn my hand to that.'

'Very good,' leered Fagin. 'Then all is agreed. You must come and visit me tomorrow. I will let you have the address.'

\*     \*     \*     \*     \*

Fagin was not in a happy mood when Noah arrived the next day. 'Dodger, my best man, has been taken from me,' Fagin informed him.

'You don't mean to say he died?' asked Noah.

'No, not as bad as that,' said Fagin. 'The Dodger was wanted by the police. They've charged him with trying to pick a pocket and they found a stolen silver snuff box on him.'

'Oh dear,' said Noah.

'Ah, he was worth fifty snuff boxes,' continued Fagin. 'You should have known the Dodger, my dear. I'd pay a pretty penny to get him back. But now they'll put him in prison for life.'

Just then Charley Bates, who had been sitting in a corner quietly, spoke. 'But young Dodger will put on a good show in court today. He won't disgrace his pals. To be jailed for life at such a young age . . . it'll be a proud moment for Dodger.'

'Aye, it will indeed,' said Fagin, cheering up a bit. 'He'll make a good speech and he'll have the court in laughter. And then we'll read all about it in the newspapers. Oh, yes, I can see the Dodger now.'

'But we must find some way of finding out what happens in court,' said Charley. 'We could send Noah to spy for us.'

Noah was not keen to go at all. In fact he was quite alarmed. 'I can't go,' he said. 'It's not my department. I'm in charge of robbing children.'

But Fagin's fearsome glare forced him to agree to undertaking the mission. Charley escorted him to the court building. 'Now you watch everything and bring us back every detail,' he said before scurrying away.

Noah walked nervously inside. The court room was dirty and the ceiling was black. It wasn't long before the Dodger was led in by the jailer. He shuffled in with his big coat sleeves tucked up as usual and took his place in the dock.

The Dodger was in a humorous mood and was clearly going to make the most of his last public appearance. 'And why, good sirs, am I placed in this disgraceful situation?' he asked mischievously.

'Hold your tongue, will you?' barked the jailer.

'I am an Englishman, ain't I?' answered Dodger. 'Where are my privileges?'

'You'll get 'em soon enough,' retorted the jailer.

'I shall thank the magistrate to dispose of my little business quickly,' said Dodger. 'I have an appointment with a gentleman in the city and I don't want to be late. So perhaps his worship would put down his newspaper and get on with the business.'

'Silence there,' shouted the jailer.

The magistrate had been so busy with his newspaper, he hadn't heard Dodger's remarks. But at that moment he stopped reading and looked up. 'What's the case?' he asked the jailer.

'Pick-pocketing, your worship.'

'Has the boy ever been before a court before?' inquired the magistrate.

'No, but he ought to have done many a time,' said the jailer. 'I know him well.'

'Where are the witnesses?' asked the magistrate.

'Yes,' said Dodger. 'Where are they? I should like to see 'em too.'

Sadly for Dodger a policeman witness stepped forward to tell how he'd seen Dodger take the snuff box.

When he had finished, the magistrate asked if Dodger had anything to say.

'No, not at the moment,' said the proud Dodger. 'But don't you worry, I will. My lawyer is having breakfast this morning with the Prime Minister and when he's ready he'll have something to say about this.'

'Take him away to prison,' said the magistrate. 'Be gone with you.'

The Dodger wasn't finished. He stared hard at the magistrate. 'It's no use you looking frightened. I won't show you any mercy. You'll pay for this. I wouldn't go free now even if you were to fall on your knees and ask me. Come, carry me off to prison.'

There was laughter around the court as Dodger was taken away.

Noah hurried back to Fagin's to give him the news that the Dodger had put on a fine show.

## Chapter Fourteen

ON the Sunday evening after her dangerous journey to see Rose, Nancy was at Sikes' house with Fagin. The clock struck eleven.

Sikes raised the window blind and looked out. 'Dark and heavy out there,' he said to Fagin. 'A good night for business.'

'It's a pity that we haven't got a job planned for tonight,' answered Fagin.

'When we've got ourselves in order again we must make up time,' said Sikes. 'Do plenty of thievin'.'

Fagin was pleased that Sikes was back in good health. 'It does me good to hear you talk like that,' he said, patting him on the arm. 'You're quite your old self again.'

Sikes shrugged his arm away. 'I don't feel like myself when you lay that withered old claw on my shoulder . . . it reminds me of being caught by the devil.'

Just then Sikes spotted Nancy putting on her bonnet.

'Hello!' cried Sikes. 'Where are you going?'

'Not far,' said Nancy.

'What sort of answer is that?' snapped Sikes. 'Where are you going? Tell me!'

'I don't know,' said Nancy.

'Then I do . . . and that's nowhere. Just you sit down again.'

Nancy pleaded with Sikes to let her go out. The nearer the clock got to midnight the more anxious she became. 'Tell him to let me go, Fagin,' she shouted, stamping her foot on the ground.

Sikes turned on her again. 'If I hear you a minute longer, the dog shall have such a grip on your throat to tear that screaming voice out. Cut my limbs off one by one, I think the gal's gone stark staring mad.'

The clock finally struck midnight and Nancy became calm again. She knew she couldn't reach London Bridge in time that night. Her head sank into her hands again.

'What's the matter with her?' said Sikes. 'I thought I had tamed her, but she's as bad as ever.'

Fagin replied that he had never seen Nancy like it before. 'Perhaps she's still got a fever,' he said.

When Fagin left to return home that night, Nancy led him to the door.

'What's wrong, Nancy?' asked Fagin. 'Is it because Sikes is such a brute to you? You know you have a friend in me. If you want revenge on someone who treats you like a dog, then come home with me. Leave him. He's a real dog. But you know me, Nance . . . I'm your friend.'

Nancy stared hard at the man who had brought her nothing but thieving and misery since she was but a child. 'I know you too well,' she said in a chilly voice. 'Goodnight.'

She closed the door and Fagin walked off towards his home. As

he darted in and out of the dim alleys, his brain was hard at work. He was convinced the girl was fed up with Sikes' brutality and was now looking for new friends. 'Why else would she want to go out alone on Sunday night?' he thought.

Fagin suddenly saw a solution to all his problems. He wanted Nancy back with him. She could be useful to him. He also wanted Sikes out of the way because he had too strong a hold on Nancy. More than that, Sikes knew too much about him and his crimes. He knew enough to have him sent to the gallows.

'With a little persuasion,' thought Fagin, 'Nancy might agree to poison him. Now, what if I discovered who her new friends were? She is terrified of Sikes and if I threatened to tell him . . . well, she would be in my power. She would do anything to stop my revealing her secrets. Aye, even poison him if I asked.'

The evil old man had decided what he was going to do by the time he got home. 'I shall have you back yet, Nance,' he mumbled fiercely.

*       *       *       *       *

Fagin was up early next morning, waiting impatiently for Noah. He arrived late and immediately demanded a huge breakfast.

'Don't you ask me anything until I have finished eating,' said Noah, whose laziness was beginning to anger Fagin. 'That's the great fault with your gang. No one gets enough time to spend on eating.'

'You can talk while you eat, can't you?' said Fagin, cursing Noah's greediness.

'Oh yes, I can do that,' said Noah, cutting a monstrous slice of bread. 'Where's Charlotte?'

Fagin explained that he'd sent her thieving with some of the gang.

'I wish you'd asked her to make some buttered toast before she left,' said Noah rudely. 'Never mind. Talk away, Mr. Fagin.'

'You did good business yesterday,' said Fagin. 'The children out on errands will be your fortune. But I want you to do a clever piece of work for me.'

Noah looked up in alarm. 'I say. Don't go shoving me into any danger. That doesn't suit me.'

'There's not the smallest danger in it,' replied Fagin. 'I only want you to follow a woman.'

Noah smiled. 'I can do that pretty well. I was a regular cunning sneak at school. What am I to follow her for?'

*As he darted in and out of the dim alleys, his brain was hard at work.*

'To tell me where she goes, who she sees and, if possible what she says.'

'What will you give me for it?' said Noah.

'If you do well,' said Fagin, 'a pound.'

Noah asked who the lady was. Fagin looked suspiciously around him and whispered: 'She's one of us.'

'Oh, lor',' cried Noah, curling up his nose. 'Don't you trust her?'

Fagin's voice became even quieter. 'She has found some new friends and I must know who they are.'

'I'm your man!' Noah said excitedly. 'Where is she? Where will I find her?'

'Just wait a while, a day or two, and I shall point her out to you.'

For six nights the cowardly spy sat awaiting Fagin's word. On the seventh, Sunday, Fagin ordered Noah to follow him. They hurried to the Three Cripples Inn.

'I'm sure she will be seeing her new friends tonight,' said Fagin entering the inn. 'Mr. Sikes has gone out and is not expected back until daybreak. So she is by herself.'

Noah followed Fagin to the small window which looked into the back room, the same place they had first met. Fagin pointed at a girl finishing a meal. It was Nancy.

'That's her,' hissed Fagin.

Noah took a hard look at the girl, who soon after got up to leave. He quickly joined Fagin in a hiding place behind a partition. Nancy came out and walked towards the inn door.

'Now follow her,' said Fagin sharply. 'Follow her and bring me news.'

Noah slid away into the night behind Nancy's hurrying figure.

## *Chapter Fifteen*

THE church clock struck a quarter to twelve as two dark figures appeared on London Bridge. One was Nancy, looking quickly about her for any sign of Rose. The other was Noah, slinking behind her in the deepest shadow he could find.

The spy followed Nancy across the bridge. Few people were about at that late time of night. A mist hung over the river, deepening the red glare from the fires burning on the moored boats. On either side of the river were huge, blackened warehouses.

Nancy reached the other end of the bridge and turned back. Noah shrank back, hiding himself behind a bridge pillar. As she passed him by, he could almost hear her breathe she was so close. After Nancy had gone on a way, Noah emerged again to follow.

The church, just visible in the gloom, tolled midnight. The ghostly chimes were still echoing when a carriage rattled to a stop at one end of the bridge. A young lady and a gentleman got out. Noah saw Nancy hurry towards them.

Nancy reached the couple. It was Rose and Mr. Brownlow. 'We can't speak here,' whispered Nancy. 'It is too public. Come down the steps over there.'

The steps led down from the bridge to a stone wharf. The river lapped at the edge. The three of them walked down, their footsteps ringing out on the stone steps.

None of them heard the hushed steps of Noah, creeping stealthily down the same path after them. He stopped where the staircase turned sharply to the right at the bottom. He could hear voices just around the corner. Noah, hidden behind a pillar, was just two paces from his prey. He listened to every word.

Nancy was speaking. 'I feel so frightened tonight, I can hardly stand.'

'What are you frightened of?' asked Mr. Brownlow.

'I don't know. All day I have felt death was following me.'

'Just imagination,' said Mr. Brownlow. 'Is it the same reason you didn't come here last Sunday night?'

'No,' said Nancy. 'I was kept at home by force – by the one I told Miss Rose about. The only reason I got away before to see Miss Rose was because I put a sleeping drug in his drink.'

Noah's eyes widened as he heard the confession.

'Now,' continued Mr. Brownlow. 'We have come here to find

out the secret of Mr. Monks. We want you to tell us how we can get to him. Just put Monks into my hands and leave us to deal with him.'

'And what if he turns against the others and tells the police about them,' said Nancy. 'Fagin and his gang are devils and worse. But I can never turn against them. I only want to help Oliver.'

Brownlow was quick to promise her that they only wanted Monks. 'If we can force the truth out of him, that's where the matter will end,' he said. 'And Monks will never learn from us that it was you who helped us to him.'

Nancy was satisfied and proceeded to tell them all she knew about Monks. She described the Three Cripples Inn and the best spot to keep a watch on it without being seen. Nancy even revealed the time when Monks normally visited the place.

'And give me his description,' said Mr. Brownlow.

'He is tall and well built, but not fat,' explained Nancy. 'He has a lurking walk, constantly looking over one shoulder and then the other. His eyes are sunk deep into his head and his face is dark. He's about twenty-eight years old . . .'

Mr. Brownlow interrupted. 'Does he have any scars?'

Nancy thought hard. 'I have only seen him once or twice and normally he is covered up with a large black cloak. But wait . . . yes . . . there is a mark on his throat.'

'A broad red mark, like a burn or a scald!' cried Mr. Brownlow excitedly.

'Yes! Yes!' said Nancy. 'You know the man.'

Rose uttered a cry of surprise.

'I think I do,' said Mr. Brownlow. 'But we shall see. Many people have similar descriptions. It may not be the same man.'

Rose and Nancy both wanted to hear more but Mr. Brownlow would not reveal another thing. Instead he turned to Nancy again. 'You have been very helpful to us. What can I do for you in return?'

'Nothing, sir,' said Nancy. 'You can do nothing to help me now. I am chained to my old life and I must return as quickly as I came. I must go home!'

Rose took out her purse and offered it to the now very frightened girl. 'Take it.'

'No,' she replied. 'I have not done this for money. If I have helped little Oliver then I have done enough. Now, goodnight, sweet lady. God bless you.'

With that, Nancy was gone, scampering up the steps and

vanishing back into the night. Soon after, Rose and
Mr. Brownlow walked to their coach and set off home.

The astonished Noah stood frozen for a few moments and then,
seeing the coast was clear, crept slowly from his hiding place. He
reached the top of the bridge and then darted off at the utmost
speed, heading for Fagin's house as fast as his long skinny legs
could carry him.

*     *     *     *     *

Noah fell fast asleep soon after telling his story to Fagin. The
old man was horrified. He sat for a long time with his face
distorted and pale, his eyes red and bloodshot. He looked less
like a man than some hideous phantom, fresh from the grave and
worried by an evil spirit.

He sat crouching over a chilly, empty hearth, wrapped in a torn
cloak. The only warmth came from a dying candle on the table.
He was biting at his black fingernails with an occasional glance at
the sleeping Noah.

Fagin was in a deadly rage. Nancy had ruined his chances of
revenge against Sikes and now he feared his game was up. The
gallows were staring him in the face again.

His black thoughts were interrupted by the sound of someone
climbing the stairs. It was still two hours before dawn, but Fagin
wasn't surprised at the early caller. It was Sikes returning from
a robbery in town, a bundle of precious items under his arm.

'I've got something to tell you,' shivered Fagin. 'Or rather
Noah, whom you don't know yet, has.'

Noah was shaken awake and hauled into a sitting position. He
rubbed his eyes and looked sleepily around him.

'Tell me your story again,' said Fagin, 'so this man here can
hear it for himself.'

Still half asleep, the young spy retold the events of the night.
Sikes, eyes glaring in disbelief, listened in silence until Noah
reached the part where Nancy had explained how she had
escaped to see Rose for the first time.

'Nancy said that a man had forced her to stay at home,' laughed
Noah, little realising who he was talking to. 'But the night she
went out to see the lady, she . . . ha! ha! ha! It made me laugh so
much when I heard it . . . she put a sleeping drug in his drink.'

Sikes leapt to his feet. 'Hell's fire,' he said, fiercely pushing
Fagin aside. 'I'm going.'

Fagin tried to stop him but Sikes' blood was up. He flung the

old man across the room and ran wildly out of the room.

'Don't be violent with her,' screamed Fagin after him. 'Be crafty. Don't get us all arrested.'

Sikes didn't hear the words. Out in the street, he ran headlong back to his own house. He opened the door quietly and crept upstairs. Once in his own room he locked the door and pushed a heavy table against it. Then he drew back the curtain around the bed.

Nancy was lying there asleep. 'Get up!' he shouted.

'Is that you, Bill?' she replied.

'It is! Get up!'

Nancy rose and, seeing the first light of dawn, stretched over to open the curtain.

'Leave it closed,' said Sikes. 'There's enough light here for what I've got to do.'

The brutal robber grabbed Nancy by the neck and dragged her into the middle of the room.

'Bill! Bill!' she gasped. 'Tell me what I've done.'

'You know what you've done, you she-devil,' snarled Sikes. 'Somebody saw you last night and heard every word you said.'

Nancy threw her arms around him, gripping the violent man strongly. 'I have been true to you, upon my life I have, you're in no danger,' she said in all honesty. 'I just wanted to help Oliver. Don't harm me . . . don't kill me . . . for your own sake don't do anything.'

Sikes' eyes were ablaze. He struggled free of Nancy's grasping arms and pulled a pistol from his pocket. He was about to fire when it flashed across his mind that the sound would bring the Bow Street Runners. Instead he brought the gun down on her head with a fearful blow.

Nancy staggered back across the room, followed by Sikes. Blind with fury, he seized a heavy club from the wall and struck her down. A pair of red eyes watched the dreadful scene from beneath the table. They belonged to the murderer's dog, Bull's-eye.

\*        \*        \*        \*        \*

It was some hours before Sikes could think straight again. He just sat in a chair, afraid to move. The hate he'd felt for what Nancy had done was now replaced by terror. He knew he would have to make a run for it; fly to a safe house.

He threw a rug over Nancy's body and walked hurriedly downstairs, Bull's-eye running behind him.

*'Don't be violent with her,' screamed Fagin after him. 'Be crafty.
Don't get us all arrested.'*

## *Chapter Sixteen*

MR. Brownlow and a servant kept watch outside the Three Cripples Inn for three days. On the fourth they saw a figure appear out of the twilight. The lurking walk and the head constantly looking back over his shoulders told Brownlow he had found his man.

The black-cloaked man moved towards the inn door, but Mr. Brownlow was there before him.

'Mr. Monks?'

The question brought Monks to a sudden halt. His head turned sharply and then the men's eyes met for the first time in many years. They recognised each other instantly, as the clever Mr. Brownlow suspected they would.

Monks' face twisted devilishly. Fear and hatred was written all over him. 'Get away from me!' he snarled. 'I want nothing to do with you.'

'I think you will come with me this instant,' said Mr. Brownlow.

'There is nothing in this world which would make me come with you,' said Monks, moving towards the door.

'Just a name,' said Mr. Brownlow confidently. 'Just a name I will mention . . . and you'll come with me.'

'What name?' snarled Monks, with equal confidence.

Mr. Brownlow moved closer and whispered two words.

\*          \*          \*          \*          \*

Later that night, Mr. Brownlow alighted from a coach at his own door. He wasn't alone. The servant and another man followed him. It was Monks.

They entered the house and climbed the stairs without speaking. At the top Monks stopped, clearly reluctant to go any further.

'You know the alternative,' said Mr. Brownlow. 'You are free to go, but if you do, we will call the police instantly. You will be arrested on a charge of fraud and robbery.'

'How dare you say these things to me,' said Monks. 'By what authority am I kidnapped in the street?'

'Well, are you going to run and face the consequences . . . or face me?' asked Mr. Brownlow.

Monks muttered under his breath. He was plainly alarmed.

'Is there no middle course?'

'None at all,' Mr. Brownlow replied sharply.

Monks shrugged his shoulders and followed Mr. Brownlow into his sitting room and sat down in a chair.

'This is nice treatment, sir,' said Monks, angrily throwing down his cloak. 'Fine treatment from my father's oldest friend.'

Mr. Brownlow's anger increased. 'It is because I was your father's oldest friend that you are here now. It's the reason why I will treat you as kindly as I can, despite all the evil you have done.'

The old gentleman leaned forward in his chair and continued in hushed tones. 'Yes, Mr. Monks . . . or shall I call you Edward Leeford. No! I cannot call you by your real name. You have brought such unworthiness to it.'

'What's in a name?' sneered Monks.

'Nothing,' said Mr. Brownlow. 'Except that I am very glad you have changed it.'

Monks looked back arrogantly. 'This is all very well, but what do you want with me?'

'You have a brother,' said Mr. Brownlow, 'a brother, a whisper of whose name caused you some alarm.'

'I have no brother,' replied Monks. 'You know I was an only child. Why do you talk of a brother?'

'Just listen to what I have to say,' said Mr. Brownlow, 'and you will hear something interesting. But first a little history. You know your father, Edwin Leeford, and your mother were not happy together.'

'Of course. They separated,' said Monks. 'They lived apart.'

'And your mother went to live abroad, taking you with her?'

'Yes. And what of it?' said Monks.

'Nothing,' replied Mr. Brownlow. 'But there is something else you know, isn't there? Your father, my good friend, Edwin, felt disgraced at his wife leaving him. But the years passed and he met new friends.'

'I know nothing of this,' said Monks, determined to deny everything.

'I think you do,' said Mr. Brownlow firmly. 'Among these new friends was a beautiful young girl. They fell in love and planned to marry.'

'Your story is very long,' said Monks, moving restlessly in his chair. 'But I will listen.'

'While you and your mother were abroad, one of your father's rich relations, who also lived abroad, died and left him a lot of money . . . a fortune, in fact.'

Monks' eyes narrowed as Mr. Brownlow continued his story. 'Your father had to travel abroad to claim the money. But no sooner had he arrived than he fell ill and died. You and your mother were with him at his death bed. His fortune went to you and your mother alone.'

Mr. Brownlow eyed Monks closely. 'That much you know.'

'What of it?' sneered Monks.

'What you didn't know was that before your father went abroad he passed through London on his way and called on me.'

'I never heard of that,' interrupted Monks, with a worried expression.

'When he came to see me he brought with him, among other things, a portrait of a young girl. He wanted me to look after it until his return. It was clear to me that it was a picture of the girl he wanted to marry.'

'Stuff and nonsense,' said Monks.

Mr. Brownlow went on: 'When I heard of your father's death I went to look for the girl but found she and her family had left her home but a week before. But why they had gone or where, no one knew.'

Monks drew breath more freely and looked up with a small smile of triumph.

'And that's an end to the story, eh?' he said.

'Sadly not,' said Mr. Brownlow. 'It just happened that your brother – the brother you deny ever existed – came to my notice. The poor, feeble and badly neglected child was taken to court after being suspected of stealing a handkerchief from me. I took pity on him and rescued him from a life of crime . . .'

'What!' cried Monks. 'What's this all about?'

'Yes,' said Mr. Brownlow. 'I told you I would say something that interested you. I did not know the boy as your brother then. But as he lay recovering in my house, his likeness to the girl in the portrait struck me with some astonishment. I saw the glimpse of an old friend in his face. But I need not tell you that the boy was snatched away from me before I could find out his history.'

'Why needn't you tell me,' said Monks hastily.

'Because you knew it well.'

'I?' Monks protested.

'You can't deny the truth. You were already in league with Fagin and paid him well to get Oliver back.'

'You . . . you . . . you can't prove anything against me,' stammered Monks. 'I defy you to do it.'

'We shall see,' said the old man with a searching glance. 'I lost the boy and no efforts of mine could discover his whereabouts. Your mother being dead, I knew that you alone could solve the mystery.'

Mr. Brownlow slowly recounted how he had travelled to the West Indies. 'After your mother's death you went there to escape the consequences of your dishonest activities. But I got there to find you had already returned to London.'

'I tried to track you down here but all I could find out was that you were living in low haunts and mingling with gangs of criminals, one Fagin among them. I paced the streets night and day but I never set eyes on you . . . until tonight!'

'And now you see me,' said Monks, rising boldly. 'What now? Fraud and robbery are high-sounding words. Do you think you can justify them just because a boy's face looked similar to a girl in a portrait? Brother! You don't even know whether the pair had a child. You don't even know that!'

'I didn't once,' replied Mr. Brownlow, getting up from his chair. 'But within the last fortnight I have learned it all. I have discovered you have a brother and that you knew it too. And what's more your father left a will which your mother destroyed. It was a will which mentioned that a child was likely to be born, wasn't it?'

'Rubbish,' said Monks. 'How could you know such things?'

'I will tell you soon enough,' continued Mr. Brownlow. 'You later went to the town where he was born looking for evidence of his birth, evidence you wanted to destroy . . . and did destroy. Remember the gold locket and wedding ring. Remember your own words to Fagin: "The only evidence of the boy's identity now lies at the bottom of the millstream".'

Monks was shocked to hear his own words repeated.

Mr. Brownlow turned on Monks: 'Now Edward Leeford . . . do you deny it now! Every word you said to that detested villain Fagin is known to me. Shadows on the wall have caught your evil whispers and brought them to my ear.'

'No! No! No!' cried the cowardly Monks, overwhelmed by the evidence.

But Mr. Brownlow wasn't finished. 'And now we hear that murder has been done to a gentle girl, Nancy, who tried to help a poor boy, your brother Oliver Twist . . . a murder for which you were partly responsible.'

'I know nothing of murder!' interrupted Monks.

'It was her revealing your secrets which led to it!'

Monks slumped back into his chair. He was a beaten man.

'Will you now write a confession before witnesses . . . the whole dreadful story?' asked Mr. Brownlow.

'If you insist,' said Monks sullenly.

'I do,' said Mr. Brownlow. 'And more too. You will remember the terms of the will your mother destroyed. You will restore Oliver's rightful share of the money to him.'

'And if I do all that . . . what then?'

'You will have one more task to complete and then you will be free to go to whatsoever part of the world you want . . . some place where we need never meet again.'

At that moment the door was opened and a servant came in. 'The murderer is close to being taken,' he cried. 'By tonight for sure!'

'Nancy's murderer?' said Mr. Brownlow.

'Yes. His dog has been seen lurking near an old haunt of his and there seems little doubt that he is there or soon will be. Spies are watching the house.'

'And what of Fagin?' asked Mr. Brownlow.

'When I last heard he had not been arrested, but he will be. The police know where he is. He can't escape.'

## Chapter Seventeen

THAT very evening Sikes had arrived back in London. His black coat and boots were thick with mud. Since taking flight from the scene of the crime, the murderer had cleared out of the city and spent days hiding in the country.

But he had been haunted by the ghost of Nancy. As he walked, he could feel her shadow following his black heels. He could hear her clothes rustling and every moaning breath of wind brought with it Nancy's last cry. Worst of all, he could see her staring eyes.

The countryside terrified him. Every shadow at night took on the appearance of some fearful object. He longed for the dark

*The countryside terrified him. Every shadow at night took on the appearance of some fearful object.*

and narrow streets of his old lairs. At last he decided to go back to London. There was a place he knew, a house where he could lay low in safety.

But before leaving the country he had looked at Bull's-eye. 'The dog!' he cursed. 'If I'm seen with him in London I'll be known in an instant.'

Sikes instantly decided he must drown the animal. He picked up a heavy stone and tied a piece of twine around it.

'Come here, Bull's-eye!' he called out.

But the dog, sensing something was wrong, backed away, cowering and growling.

'Come here!' shouted Sikes, angrily stamping his foot on the ground.

The dog wagged its tail but didn't move. Sikes darted forward to grab hold of him. But the frightened animal turned and ran off.

He cursed Bull's-eye as the dog vanished on the road towards the city.

Sikes waited on the outskirts of London until the night was at its darkest and most people were in bed. Then he padded quickly towards his destination, a miserable haunt on the River Thames called Jacob's Island.

There was nowhere in London so desolate. Only the poorest people and criminals lived there. The streets ran between tottering house fronts. Chimneys leaned in the air ready to fall to the ground. Rusty iron bars guarded rotting windows. Filth littered the streets.

In an upper room of one of those houses, ruined but heavily defended by bars at the door and window, sat two men. There was Toby Crackit, who had been with Sikes on the robbery at Mrs. Maylie's house, and an old thief called Kags. His nose had been flattened at one time in a scuffle and his face had a fearful scar. They were discussing some dramatic events which had happened earlier that evening.

'When was Fagin took by the police?' asked Kags.

'I was there when they came,' said Toby. 'Charley Bates and I made a quick escape up the wash-house chimney. The new man, Noah, tried to hide by diving into an empty water barrel. But his legs were so long they stuck out and the police took him too.'

'What's become of Charley?' asked Kags.

'He'll be here soon,' said Toby. 'But not Fagin. He'll be in jail with the rest of the crew from the Cripples Inn. The officers fought like the devil to take 'em all. The evidence is all there . . . Fagin will hang within six days.'

The men were thinking about the gloomy situation when they heard a pattering sound on the stairs. Bull's-eye bounded into the room.

'How the devil did he get in?' said Kags. 'Must have jumped through a window.'

'What does it mean?' said Toby. 'Sikes can't be coming here. I . . . I . . . I hope not.'

'If he was coming he would have come with the dog,' Kags pointed out.

'Old Bull's-eye must be looking for his master,' said Toby. 'The old dog has been to this place often enough with him.'

Bull's-eye crept under a chair and went to sleep. Soon after there was a knock at the door.

'See who it is before you let 'em in, Toby,' said Kags.

Toby went downstairs and peered through a crack in the door. A white face with sunken eyes, hollow cheeks and a newly grown beard met his anxious stare. It was Sikes.

They hurried upstairs and Sikes glared at Bull's-eye. 'How did he get here?'

Before anyone could answer there was another knock at the door. Toby went down again and reappeared with Charley Bates, who spotted Sikes immediately.

'Charley!' said Sikes, making as if to shake his hand. 'Glad to see you again.'

'Don't come near me!' snapped Charley. 'Nancy's murderer. You monster. If the police come after you here I'll give you up to them. I promise you I will.'

Charley began shouting at the top of his voice for help and then threw himself at Sikes. Charley was only a thin boy but he tumbled Sikes to the ground. They were rolling around on the ground when Toby Crackit called out in alarm, pointing out of the window.

There were lights gleaming below and the tramp of hurried footsteps. Then came a loud knock at the door.

'Help!' shrieked Charley. 'He's up here. Sikes is here!'

'In the King's name, open this door!' came the reply. Immediately after came the sound of men battering at the door.

Sikes ran to the window and looked down. A huge mob had gathered beneath. They were shouting and urging the police to break the door down. Sikes menaced the crowd with his fists and shouted down: 'Do your worst. I'll cheat you yet!'

Sikes turned and shouted at Toby. 'Give us a rope . . . a long one!'

The panic-stricken Toby quickly found one and Sikes ran to a room at the back of the house. He squeezed through a window and clambered onto the roof.

Forty feet below was a wide muddy ditch and on the other side of it, a row of ramshackle houses. Soon faces appeared at the windows and clusters of onlookers peered up towards Sikes. 'They have him now!' hissed the mob.

Sikes sank back for a moment, frightened by the ferocity of the crowd. Then he sprang to his feet again. He tied one end of the rope around a chimney stack, and the other into a noose loop. Sikes was going to let himself down to the ditch.

He put the rope over his head and was about to slip it beneath his armpits when something attracted his attention. Sikes turned and looked behind him on the roof. He threw his hands up and let out a yell of terror.

'The eyes again!' he screamed. 'Nancy's eyes!'

Staggering as if struck by lightning, he lost his balance and tumbled over the edge of the roof. The noose was at his neck. He fell for thirty feet and then the rope ran out.

The old chimney shook but stood the strain. Below the murderer swung lifeless against the wall.

The eyes, glinting red from the lights opposite, moved again. Bull's-eye, who had clambered onto the roof, let out a dismal howl. He gathered himself to jump for the dead man's shoulders. Missing Sikes' body he tumbled into the ditch below and striking his head against a stone, died instantly.

## Chapter Eighteen

THE day after Sikes' death, Oliver found himself in a carriage rolling fast towards the town where he was born. Rose, Mrs. Maylie and Mrs. Bedwin were with him. Mr. Brownlow was delayed on some important business and would follow them a little later.

*Staggering as if struck by lightning, he lost his balance and tumbled
over the edge of the roof.*

They had not talked much on the way. Oliver was in such a state of agitation and uncertainty. Mr. Brownlow had told them in the briefest outline what he had forced out of Monks. But still the matter was wrapped in enough doubt and mystery to leave them in dreadful suspense.

As they neared the town, Oliver began to see landmarks of old times; a crowd of emotions filled his head.

'See there, there!' cried Oliver, eagerly grasping Rose's hand and pointing out of the carriage window. 'That's the stile I came over after running away from Mr. Sowerberry; there are the hedges I crept behind in case anyone should see me. Look! That's the path that leads to the old house where I was a little child. Oh, Dick, my dear old friend. I wonder how he is. If only I could see him now.'

'You will soon,' said Rose, holding his hand. 'You shall tell him how happy you are. And you'll make him happy too.'

'Yes, yes,' said Oliver. 'We'll take him away from here and look after him. We'll take him away, have him clothed and taught, and send him to a nice place in the country . . . and there he will grow strong and well . . . oh, shall we, Rose?'

Rose nodded and hugged him. There were tears in Oliver's eyes, such happy ones.

They drove into the town and Oliver was so excited. There was Sowerberry's the coffin-maker's place, and there was the workhouse with its dismal windows frowning on the street. The carriage pulled up at the biggest hotel. In the old days Oliver used to stare at it in awe, thinking it was a palace.

They all sat down to dinner, but Mr. Brownlow, who had arrived soon after, didn't join them. He sat in another room, poring over some papers with another man.

When the clock struck nine o'clock everyone at dinner began to think they would hear no more secrets that night. But suddenly the door opened and Mr. Brownlow walked in, accompanied by a man.

Oliver let out a shriek of surprise. 'That's the man who frightened me in the town,' he cried out. 'He was with Fagin looking at me through the window.'

'Yes, I know now,' said Mr. Brownlow. 'This is your brother, Oliver, the man I spoke to you about.'

Monks cast a look of pure hatred at the astonished boy and sat down by the door.

'This child, as you will know,' said Mr. Brownlow, turning to Monks, 'is your brother, your half brother. He is the son of your father by poor young Agnes Fleming, who died after giving birth to him. That is correct, is it not?'

'Yes,' said Monks, scowling at the boy. 'That is their child.'

'He was born in the workhouse of this town?' said Mr. Brownlow.

'Yes,' replied Monks sullenly. 'You have the whole story in your hand.' He pointed to the papers Mr. Brownlow was carrying.

'I have your signed confession,' said Mr. Brownlow. 'But I want these good people to hear it in your own words.'

'All right then,' said Monks, angrily. 'When my father died abroad, my mother and I were with him. Among his papers was a letter to the girl Agnes and a will.'

'What did the letter say?' asked Mr. Brownlow.

'He prayed to her that she wouldn't curse his memory if he died before they could marry. He reminded her of some trinkets he had given her, a locket and a ring with her Christian name engraved upon it.'

'And the will?' said Mr. Brownlow.

Monks fell silent and so Mr. Brownlow continued the story for him. 'In the will, your father spoke of you as an evil and bad son. But he still left eight hundred pounds to you and your mother. The bulk of the property was to be divided between Agnes Fleming and her child, should it be born alive. The will also said that if the child ever did wrong or fell into criminal ways, then all the money should go to you.'

'That's right,' growled Monks. 'My mother burned the will and the letter was never sent. She kept it. I was very young at the time, but when my mother died she gave it to me and told me the story of the will. She was certain that Agnes had given birth to a boy and I swore to hunt it down. Fagin has the letter now.'

'And the locket and the ring?' asked Mr. Brownlow.

'I bought them from the man and woman I told you of. You know what became of them . . . lost at the bottom of the stream.'

Mr. Brownlow left the room for a second and returned shortly afterwards with Mrs. Bumble, who in turn was dragging in her unwilling husband.

'Do my eyes deceive me!' cried Mr. Bumble. 'Oh, Oliver, if you knew how much I have missed you.'

'Hold your tongue, fool!' hissed Mrs. Bumble.

'Why, no, my dear,' he continued. 'I have always loved that boy as if he were my own. You remember, don't you, dear Oliver.'

Mr. Brownlow ignored Mr. Bumble's lies and pointed at Monks. 'Do you know this man?'

'Never saw him in all my life,' said Mr. Bumble.

'Never,' said Mrs. Bumble flatly.

Brownlow stared hard at them. 'You never had, perhaps, a certain gold locket and ring?'

'Certainly not!' replied Mrs. Bumble. 'Why have you brought us here?'

Monks spoke again. 'You might as well tell them. I have confessed all.'

'If this man has been coward enough to confess,' said Mrs. Bumble, 'then I have nothing more to say. I did sell 'em and they are where you'll never find 'em again. So there! What now?'

'Nothing,' replied Mr. Brownlow, 'but for us to make sure that neither of you ever enjoys a job of importance again.'

Mr. Bumble was trembling and sweating. 'I do hope,' he said, 'that this unfortunate matter will not deprive me of my job as Master of the workhouse.'

'Indeed it will!' said Mr. Brownlow. 'Now you may leave the room.'

'It was all Mrs. Bumble's fault,' cried Mr. Bumble. 'She wanted to do it.'

Mr. Brownlow gave him a quick lesson in law. 'The law says that your wife acted under your direction.'

'Then the law is an ass,' snapped Mr. Bumble, putting on his hat and leaving the room with his dreadful wife.

Mr. Brownlow turned to Monks again. 'We are getting to the end of the story,' he said, 'but there is more. Rose, give me your hand. Don't tremble. You have nothing to fear from the few remaining words.'

Rose looked very puzzled but put her hand in his.

Mr. Brownlow spoke to Monks again. 'Your mother came to England before she died, didn't she? To search for Agnes.'

'Yes,' said Monks. 'Agnes' father had taken his family and left the area. But my mother kept searching and found out the whole story. She traced the family to Wales.'

'What did she find?' asked Mr. Brownlow.

'Agnes' father had died and Agnes herself had vanished.'

'We know more of that, don't we?' said Mr. Brownlow. 'Agnes was then on her way towards London. Heartbroken at the death of your father, she wanted to visit his grave. She intended travelling abroad.'

'Yes,' said Monks. 'You know the rest.'

'Poor Agnes didn't get there,' said Mr. Brownlow. 'She reached the workhouse of this town, exhausted and very ill. And there she died after giving birth to Oliver.'

A tear formed in Oliver's eye as Mr. Brownlow grasped Rose's hand even tighter. 'Now, just one more thing,' he said. 'Monks, do you know this young lady?'

'Yes,' he replied.

Rose felt faint. 'But I have never seen him before,' she said.

Mr. Brownlow continued: 'Monks, when your mother visited Wales, she didn't find Agnes but she discovered another child of the family. Agnes had a sister.'

'Yes,' said Monks. 'She was living with a poor family who had taken her in. She had no one left in the world to look after her. But she didn't stay with that family. A wealthy lady saw the child, took pity on her and gave her a home. My mother found out who the lady was and told me about her before she died.'

'When did you last see Agnes' sister?' asked Mr. Brownlow.

'I lost sight of her two or three years ago and I saw no more of her until recently,' said Monks. 'That was soon after the time I bumped into Oliver in the town near Mrs. Maylie's home.'

'Do you see her now?' asked Mr. Brownlow. Everyone looked up, very surprised indeed.

'Yes,' said Monks. 'She's leaning on your arm!'

Rose ran to Mrs. Maylie and almost fainted in her arms. 'My heart will burst with happiness,' she cried. 'I can hardly bear it.'

Mrs. Maylie embraced her tenderly and then turned her towards Oliver. 'Come, come, my dear,' she said. 'Remember who wants to hug you too. See there, look, my dear.'

Oliver, so astonished by the news, had been frozen to the spot for a second. Now he went to Rose and threw his arms around her neck.

'My mother's sister.' he cried. 'Darling Rose, you are my aunt . . . oh, but I can never call you aunt . . . you will always be my own dear sister.'

A father, sister and mother were gained . . . and lost . . . in that moment. Joy and sadness mingled together as the two orphans cried together.

## *Chapter Nineteen*

Aand so the story of Oliver Twist is nearly ended. It only remains to tell what happened afterwards to the little orphan boy and the characters who played a part in his childhood.

The morning after Mr. Brownlow's revelations, Mrs. Maylie came down to find Oliver crying quietly on the stairs. 'Oliver, my child,' she said. 'Why are you so sad? What's the matter?'

Oliver's face said it all. He had gone out earlier on a visit to the paupers' nursery. He wanted to see the friend he had never forgotten.

But poor Dick was dead.

\*        \*        \*        \*        \*

Oliver's last unhappy task was to recover his father's letter which Monks had given to Fagin for safe-keeping. Oliver journeyed to London with Mr. Brownlow. Their destination was the infamous Newgate prison.

Fagin, brought to court and sentenced by the judge to hang for all his many evil crimes, was there already.

His last home was the condemned man's cell. The only furniture was a stone bench, a mattress and an iron candlestick fixed into the cold stone wall. A tiny barred window allowed a little daylight to filter down to the floor.

As his last day quickly passed, Fagin sat thinking of all the men he had known to have died on the gallows, many of them because of him. He shivered when he thought how a strong man could suddenly become a heap of dangling clothes.

It was the Sunday evening when Oliver and Mr. Brownlow arrived. Fagin had one night left to live.

At the prison gate they were met by a jailer. 'Surely the young man should not be faced with Fagin,' he said, pointing to Oliver. 'He is not a sight for children.'

Mr Brownlow agreed but added: 'This boy has seen the man in all his villainy. I think it right that he should see him now.'

They were led into the prison and taken down some narrow steps which descended into a stone corridor. On one side there was a row of strong and bolted doors. The jailer stopped at one of them and unlocked it.

Fagin was sitting on a stone bench, rocking himself from side to side. Around his head was a bandage. He had been wounded during his capture.

'Fagin!' shouted the jailer. 'Somebody wants to see you to ask you some questions.'

The old man caught sight of Oliver and Mr. Brownlow. 'What do you want?' he asked, shrinking back.

'You have a letter,' said Mr. Brownlow. 'It was placed in your safe-keeping by a man called Monks.'

'It's a lie. I haven't,' protested Fagin.

'It's no good,' said Mr. Brownlow. 'Monks has confessed everything. You have nothing to lose. Monks told us you have it. Where is it?'

'Come here, Oliver,' whispered Fagin. 'Let me whisper to you.'

Oliver reluctantly let go of Mr. Brownlow's hand and moved closer to Fagin. 'The letter,' he said, 'is in a canvas bag hidden in a hole in my chimney. You know the one!'

'Yes,' said Oliver, trembling a little.

Fagin hadn't finished. 'Now, I have helped you, you must help me. Come take me away from this place. I am an old man, a very old man. Take me away from here.'

Oliver looked at Fagin. He had suffered so much at the hands of the old man but even now he felt sorry for him. 'God forgive him,' cried Oliver.

'Yes, God forgive me, my dear,' said Fagin. 'Now help me to the door.'

Fagin was in a dream and began walking towards the door. 'Come on Oliver, press on, Take me with you. If I tremble as we pass the gallows, don't worry. Just hurry on and get me out of this prison.'

The jailer put his hands on Fagin's shoulder. The old man struggled with the power of desperation but finally his strength gave up. He sank to the floor and let out a terrible cry. Oliver and Mr. Brownlow left and the heavy cell door clanged shut.

*       *       *       *       *

So ended Fagin's life. But what of the others?

Before three months had passed, Rose was married to a young man in the village where Mrs. Maylie lived. The old lady lived out the rest of her days happily with them.

Monks, still using his false name, sailed for America. He soon fell into bad ways again and ended up in prison. That is where he died.

Noah Claypole received a free pardon for giving evidence

against Fagin and the other members of the gang. He and Charlotte stayed together and began a new business; they became police informers.

Mr. and Mrs. Bumble lost their jobs. As the years passed, they became very poor. They finally became paupers in the very same workhouse where they had once lorded it over others. But Mr. Bumble was often heard to say how glad he was that he didn't have to live in the same room as his wife.

The Dodger was transported to a prison in Australia. He never lost his chirpy spirit and kept all his fellow inmates amused with his cocky antics. He returned to England an old man to live with his friend and partner, Charley Bates.

Charley, so horrified by Nancy's murder, began to think an honest life might be better after all. He spent a short time in prison and then became a farmer's labourer. He worked hard and saved all his money. Charley finally bought some land and became a successful farmer himself.

Mr. Brownlow, who had been the first person to show Oliver any kindness, completed the boy's happiness by adopting him as his son. The old man, Mrs. Bedwin and Oliver went to live in the same village as Rose.

They shared such happy days together. Mr. Brownlow filled Oliver's mind with his great store of knowledge and he grew more and more fond of the boy.

They were regular visitors at Rose's home. And Oliver still gathered wild flowers for her every morning in summer. But he could never call her 'aunt'.

'She will always be a sister to me,' he would say, 'because she loves me like a brother.' Oliver and Rose were truly happy at last.

In the village church a white marble stone was placed on a wall by the altar. It bore a simple inscription: 'IN MEMORY OF AGNES'.

The memory of Oliver's mother lingered long in that quiet nook. There Oliver and Rose, her gentle hand on his shoulder, would often be found in silent thought . . . the two orphans together.

*THE END*